I0456829

THE LEZORY FILES, (A Lesbian Story)

Authors, Rose Sutra and Safari Ann Jones

Copyright 2006, TX 6-504-204

Edited by Rose Sutra

Published by Rose Sutra and Safari Ann Jones

ISBN 978-0-61514727-7

About the Authors:

This is a nonfiction autobiography lesbian story told by two women of color. There are always two sides to a story. Rose Sutra was born in Harlem New York, and Safari Ann Jones was born in Ohio. We wrote this material in hopes of sharing with the world how we feel about being in the Life. Sometimes the Life is not all what it seems. This literature is packed with many shocking stories stemming from childhood, one-nightstands, parties-n-bullshit, and having long-term relationships with other women. This story will make you laugh hysterically or cry like heavy raindrops during a hot summers day.

Safari Ann Jones is a native of Ohio who has spent a majority of her life living the military life. Safari lived a Majority of her life in states such as Ohio, California, Chicago, Florida and Virginia. The constant moving uprooting of her life by her Father's career caused Safari to frantically search all of her life for stability, acceptance and success. The daughter of a military man and a loving hard working mother, Safari experienced life in her own unique way. The youngest of three siblings, Safari was destined for a bright future but life just kept getting in the way. Most of the time taking the turn for the worst, but the adventure of life has kept Safari moving when life was hard and hurtful. Through strength and perseverance, Safari has blossomed from a lost naive, unhappy child, starved of attention to a full-fledged lesbian woman, and humanitarian who loves life and herself now. Safari Ann Jones has appeared on the Montel William's show, Emerald cove, a French television and on the Oprah Winfrey show. As a teenager, Safari dreamed of being a famous singer and supermodel. Safari wanted to travel the world and was signed to a modeling contract with a local agency after a talent search. Safari has not forgotten her dreams and still shoots for the stars, to hopefully someday find the missing pieces of her life. For right now, Safari is content with just being happy, healthy and full of life. Safari Ann Jones is the survivor of three Florida hurricanes along with her lover and partner Rose. Safari has also survived numerous abusive relationships, yet she still lives and thrives in the hearts and minds of many. Safari Ann Jones still has the ability to do one thing without a dream. A person loses the will to live but Ms. Jones has a lot more living to do. So she chooses live on.

Through the eyes of wide-eyed child, Safari is embraced and blessed by the spirits of her courageous grandmothers in heaven. The love they gave Safari keep her a God fearing soul. She is at peace. Her heart and mind are humble now.

Introduction:

The literature presented in this book is geared towards the betterment of lesbians across the Diaspora. What you will read is insanely graphic, hysterically funny, terribly sad, and humanly true. Both writers write out of hurt, pain, fear, desire, love and joy. Lesbianism, humanitarism, and consciousnism equal the life style in their eyes of being gay. The Lezory Files, (A Lesbian Story), portrays two African American females that meet and fall in love, in spite of their trials and tribulations they face and have faced apart and together. Safari was born in Ohio, and Rose was born in Harlem, New York. They find each other in Orlando Florida. Are they past life lovers, or lifetime mates? Continue reading and you will discover the answer. Safari and Rose are two women that are learning from each other. To quote Rose, "We are women and we learn from women, how to love women."

The pages are packed with sex, lies and humongous drama titled, Childhood shapes the woman, "Parties-N-Bullshit," "My One-Nightstands," "Long-Term Relationships," and "Flashbacks To The Times We Had," are relevant to societies psychological mechanisms of thought that provoke us to portray many different roles and characters, throughout our life span on this planet. We as women need more nurturing within the womb before exiting our mothers birth canal. Some ladies choose to be

4

lesbians and some were born that way. To quote Safari, "I am straight." "I am not a lesbian, I choose to be with women therefore, I am a choosebian". To quote Rose, "I am a lesbian, and I was born this way." "At this point in my life, I would not ever go back to men." "I am a lesbian for life." Meaning, a lesbian lifer! As one can see, both authors come from two different mindsets, but they enjoy a happy medium, to share one common ground, towards building a safe, kind, loving, and trusting relationship in the hands of the most high. All names have been changed to protect the innocent.

TABLE OF CONTENTS

CHAPTER I

IMAGES OF REMINESE

By, Rose Sutra

Images of reminisce...

Thinking about my first tongue kiss.

And when momma beat me because I disobeyed her first wish.

And when papa sat me down on his lap and told me about all this madness.

And then told me to guard my twat against many brothers trying to enter it.

And, not to get pregnant before I was married.

Yeah, I got many images of reminisce... But as I grew, I tried not to act like the slave that my grandma told me that she once knew.

So I fought hard to release those chains from my brain, as the most high shocked my memory.

And showed me visions took me on journeys through history, and her story. It's a thin line between love and hate.

Then building me on another higher level of mentality, with the angelic spirits coaching and guiding me spiritually.

And the deities directing me holistically, striving strategically to maintain this great legacy.

Yeah, I got many images of reminisce.

You see I just can't forget.

Brothers tried physically too rape me for the jewel between my legs gee!

Sisters trying to steal from me the man by my side see!

Eventually the brother left me.

I got so fed-up with the male species, that I tried the experience of being a lesbian.

Thinking that would heal the pain of the male hypocrisy!

But little did I know that the childhood pain stemmed inside of me.

SO WHAT'S UP GOD?

Because a sister like me is down her knees.

Asking for forgiveness from the almighty!

To release me from the madness!

You see I'm going back to when papa sat me on his knee and schooled me about societies shit before it hit. Because, now I'm at the age of?

"Dam"

Yeah, I got many images of reminisce.

CHILDHOOD SHAPES THE WOMAN

By, Rose Sutra

Telling my lezory, meaning a lesbian story. The drama began when my mother read about my dirty lesbian act at seventeen. Yeah, moms read my diary and apparently at her age, and with her cultural back round, and up bringing, she did not agree with my life style. I walked in the house early Sunday evening after hanging out all day with my best friend Noël. I walked in the house all happy as usual and headed straight up stairs to my bedroom. As I walked in my room, my mother charged at me with a butcher knife saying, "You will not be a lesbian living in my house." "We did not raise you like that." It seemed like that all she saw was red, not a daughter, person or a human being. She totally freaked and lost it. If my father did not pull her off of me, I would have not written this story that you are reading today. My moms, Doreen Wilson, was raised as a Catholic, Guyanese, American woman. She was from the old school, where there was no such thing as being gay or lesbian. She was unaccustomed to this type of behavior.

At this point, my moms was yelling, and screaming, "My daughter is not a lesbian," Spit shooting from her mouth and my Father, Jason Wilson yelling at my moms saying, "Have you lost your mind baby?" "You are going to kill the child." My father pulled her off of me and took her down stairs to calm her down. They both left my room disgusted and angry.

How did I feel? Angry, hurt, exposed, surprised, violated, shocked, degraded and abandoned. My mother was my best friend, other than my childhood best friend Noël. I was used to getting beatings, but not like this. My moms took me everywhere with her. I said to myself, how could she? Was she on drugs? So what if I was getting it on with my best girl friend? It was none of her business. Let me live my life.

Two hours later, I found out that my mother had called Noël's mother, and told her that Noël and I were lesbians. As if? Who wants to hear this about their own daughter? Now, you knew Noël had to call and tell me. "Is your mother tripping or what?" Why would she sneak and read my diary? I guess because I stopped talking to her for about two months. Well, I was in the process of getting turned out by my best friend! I did not leave my diary out. My mother deliberately searched for it. She found it under my mattress. There, she found my entire dirty little lesbian thoughts and escapades.

While Noël and I talked on the phone she said, "how did your mother find out about you and me?" I said, "My mother searched my entire room and found my diary and read it." Noël said, "Your mother did that, oh shit." I said, "Yeah, she knows every thing." Noël said, "Why did you keep a diary?" I told her that I have always had a diary that I wrote in everyday. Noël said, " Rose you need to burn that diary." I replied, "Burn my diary, heck no!" This diary contained all my thoughts and feelings, how could I burn that away. But the next Saturday, Noël came over my house while my parents were gone and we watched my diary burn to ashes in the back yard of my parent's home.

Did Noël and I remain friends, yes, lovers, no. After high school we parted and went our separate ways. I really loved her, but she cheated on me with another Spanish woman. At the time I was bisexual. Noël had said to me to make a choice between men or women. At the time, I felt I did not have to make a choice. I did not make choice but she did.

ROSE 6

Ass fucking for me stemmed from being molested at six years old. One day, Net the babysitter left me with her nephew Brice. Brice was eighteen, tall, thin; light skinned, short black hair and a heavy voice. If I were seventeen, I would have thought he was cute. When Net left me alone with Brice, he took me into Net's room and said, "Let's play house." "I will be the husband and you will be the wife." He proceeded to take my hand and guide me towards the bed and pull back the sheets. He told me to get in the bed and take off all my cloths. I said, "no." He said, "If you don't I will tell Net that you was bad, and you will get spanked." So, I took off my cloths, because I did not want to get beat. He turned the television on and laid beside me. He started touching all over my body. He told me to touch his penis, I did and it felt long, and hard. At six years of age you don't know what you are doing. He got on top of me and started poking his penis into my small vagina. He did that for about fifteen minutes or so. He then told me to open my mouth and stuck his penis into my mouth and told me to suck it. I said, "No." Brice said, "I am going to tell Net you have been bad." So, I started to suck his penis. He then told me to stop and let's go to the bathroom. He told me to get into the bathtub. I did. He got into the bathtub after me, and told me to turn around with my ass facing him. He told me to bend over. I did. He started to ram his penis into my anus. This type of behavior went on till my family moved to Brooklyn New York. I had never told anyone. So, ass fucking for me became a pleasure, a delicacy, as I grew older!

Life progressed, and I now was eighteen and graduating from high school. I met some very important people that would play key roles in my life. I was still bisexual and loving it. I felt life was just beginning. I met Tiesha, who was my first rap partner. We signed in and out of two recording contracts together. We were signed to Doug E Fresh's ex manager, Denise Bell. At the time we did several shows, and recorded some records. We also got jerked. Between all the record label dramas, I had met several women. This is where my lezory begins.

CHILDHOOD SHAPES THE WOMAN

SAFARI

I can still remember four years old in the hot summer of Ohio and I had my prettiest bows and ribbons in my hair and my sunflower yellow dress with the little white ruffles on the bottom and my yellow sandals that big granny bought me. Today was the first day of summer. A day I would always remember. My name is Safari Ann Jones but everybody calls me Fari. My mamma calls me Fari Ann and Annie pooh but I answer to them all. I have a big brother named, James Dwayne and boy is he nosey and is always getting whippings from mama cause he is just bad. I love my big sister Kyzelle. She is the best big sister in the whole world. She buys me toys and treats. She never makes me eat dirt like that Mean ole James. James Dooley and Jeff are shooting marbles and Kyzelle and all of her friends are rehearsing for the summer talent show. I am so bored. I skipped in the house and yelled "Maaaama! Mamma! Can I go to Lashay's house?" Mamma said "yes, but be back before the street lights come on or imma heat that hiney and don't let that little fast tail girl get you in any trouble or you are going to get it!" "Ok mamma" I said. So I got on my big wheel and off I went to Shay Shay's house. Shay Shay's house was the tallest brick house on the street and it always looked busy. I parked my big wheel and stood on my tippy toes to try to ring the bell and finally I reached it. I waited and waited and finally the biggest blackest woman I have ever seen answered the door. I was so scared of this woman that I almost ran. She had on this dirty white robe with matching slippers and big pink rollers with the white pins in them. This big scary woman had the phone to her ear and was talking a gazillion miles a minute. I don't think she took a breath. Finally she said, "Hold on Claudine." "Fari Ann is you looking for LaShay?" I said, "Yes maam." She said, "Well come on in child, she is down that hallway and on the left." I started walking. I tell ya Shay's house was the funkiest house ever! It smelled like those funny cigarettes and baby pee pee diapers mixed in! I walked halfway down the hallway and then I stopped. Mrs. Jackson stared at me as I walked down the hallway and looked at me in the strangest way. I was only four and I couldn't remember which side was left, so I started doing the hokey pokey just like my big sis Kyzelle taught me, so I could remember my left from my right. Mrs. Jackson yelled, "Child what the hell are you doing?" I said " The hokey pokey." She said, "Claudine these damn children dun lost their minds." I heard "Fari, Fari in here". I opened the door and there was Shay and she said close the door before the boys see my booty. I stood near the door trying not to look but it was hard when she was sitting on the toilet with her pink little lace dress on with her matching frilly socks and her white frilly panties around her ankles. I looked around and saw roaches scurrying around and dirty clothes everywhere. Mamma would have a fit if our house looked and smelled this bad. Shay Shay said, "Come here Safari." I slowly walked towards Shay. I walked as slow as I could because I knew that Shay Shay was sometimes trouble. Last week she made me eat worms and kiss that old ugly Jaton Tucker. Shay Shay stood up from the toilet and told me to kneel on the floor. I did what I was told because Shay was pretty smart. I mean she was almost seven years old and seven year olds are way smarter than four year olds. She said, "Close your eyes Fari." I closed my eyes and she said, "Lick out your tongue." I licked out my tongue. I just knew a worm or some dirt was coming. I felt something warm and wet. I opened my eyes and my tongue was on Shay Shay's private part. She had one foot on the toilet and one on the floor. She was spreading her cootie bird wide open! She had her eyes closed and she was saying, "Ooh baby lick it." I just kept licking and I remember my head being under her little frilly dress. I thought it was hot and her cootie bird tasted like slimy wet salt. Finally Shay said, "Fari you can get up now and you better not tell anyone what you did cause your mamma and my mamma will beat us." I said, "I promise I wont tell." I remember that day I just wiped my face with my arm and I ran out the front door and got on my big wheel and peddled away. I thought to myself "Why did Shay want me to lick her cootie?" I never did understand that and I just thought well maybe she had some bad itch or something. I never thought about that moment again. Years later, I realized that my moment with Shay Shay had formed the rest of my life. This is where my lezory begins. But, I was too young to know or care about the journey that I was about to embark on.

SAFARI 10

I am ten years old and I live in California now. I loved the California sun
and watching my friend that I secretly liked a lot. Her name was Maxelle.
Max was the coolest girl I knew. Her mother was from China and her dad
was Black. Maxell was so pretty with her jet-black curls and her muscular
arms and legs. She was a gymnast. I thought she was the coolest, because
she could do back flips. I could sit in the grass and pick dandelions all day
and watch Max do flips and splits. One day, Max and I were at my house
playing and she said, "Lets play first date" I said, "What's that?" She said,
"You have to be the man and I will be the woman." "We will pretend we
are going out to dinner and then we will go home." I said, "Ok" We
pretended to eat dinner then Max said, "Ok time to go to the house and she
laid on the bed and said, "Ok now you got to hump me." I said, "Why?"
She said, "Well that is what men and women do." So me being the naïve,
I proceeded to hump and grind. Then Michelle said, "Now kiss my lips at
the same time." Just as I started kissing her, my big mouth brother James
ran in said, "Oooh Fari and Max!" "I am going to tell mamma and she is
going to beat you silly." I started to cry and said, "James please don't tell
mamma, I don't want no spanking." I bribed James with my secret stash of
candy and my new bag of cat's eye marbles, so he wouldn't tell. That day,

I knew I liked kissing girls. I also knew that it was not ok, and it could get you into a world of trouble. So I vowed to never do it again.

SAFARI LOVES TYRANN

When I was about twelve I had a friend named Tyrann. She was so spoiled. She also was the baby of her family just like me. Yet, I wasn't spoiled and she was spoiled rotten. Tyrann had some of the biggest juiciest lips that I had ever seen. She had an older sister named Berrin that Tyrann ordered around. It was so cool that Tyrann could boss her big sister, and I was pretty amazed. Kyzelle would've slapped me into the middle of next week if I tried to boss her around. I knew Kyzelle was the boss when mama wasn't home, so I just dreamed of being like Tyrann. Tyrann had every toy, video game and clothing fit for a queen. I loved hanging at Tyrann's house that is until her snooty friend Cecily Whitenmore came over. I hated Cecily because she was twelve going on twenty-four. Her father waited on her mother hand and foot, just because she was a light skinned trophy wife. In Virginia, light skin means status and almost white which equaled snooty and uppity in my book. Cecily was this light skinned longhaired princess from hell. She took baths and facials at least five times a day everyday and changed her clothes like the wind. Cecily always dressed like Cinderella or the royal queen. One night, Cecily went home sick and our friend Christina or "White Chocolate" as we called her.

She was sleeping on the floor with ding-dong Gracie. Gracie was really stupid. So we called her ding-dong. We felt sorry for Gracie. We were her friends just so we could get into heaven for doing a good deed. Tyrann and I were in the bed sleeping. Well at least she was sleeping. I don't know why? But I just couldn't sleep on her satin sheets. The sheets were pretty, cold and slippery. I peeked under the covers and started to giggle. Tyrann had a big ole butt and I was staring at it. Everyone made fun of her butt and the boys liked to squeeze it and run away. I don't know what came over me that night. I kept peeking under the covers and staring at her butt. My private part began to tingle and pulsate. I quietly scooted closer and closer to her butt and pretended to stretch, so I could get nearer to Tyrann. An hour later, I was lying up against Tyrann's butt and it felt really good. I wanted to wrap my arms around her, but I was afraid that she would roll over and slap me, so I barely breathed or moved. Something came over me, and for some reason, I wanted to touch her butt with my hand. The thought made my privates really moist and hot. I didn't know why I was feeling this way about my friend, but I knew it felt good. Slowly I reached out to touch Tyrann's juicy butt and I gave it a rub and a little squeeze. I rested my hand on her left butt cheek and she didn't move. All of a sudden she grabbed my hand and my heart stopped. I was busted and I knew it! To my surprise, Tyrann put my hand down her pants and whispered squeeze it all you want. I did. I was so embarrassed that I pretended to drift off to sleep. We never spoke of this incident again and pretended nothing ever happened. Secretly I had a crush on Tyranny and I never told her.

SWEET SAFARI'S SAD SEVENTEEN

At seventeen years old, I decided that church was my life. I was on the usher's board and I sang in at least four choirs. I swear my mother and I went to church at least five days a week. I tell ya with all of my church going, I am definitely promised to go to heaven or at least have a spot in heaven's Baptist church choir! All my life I was taught that being a good girl and keeping my legs closed would keep me safe and would get me into heaven. I didn't have a boyfriend until I was at least 19 years old. My mother set us up. There was this nice boy that liked me from the church choir and his name was Benny Poe. Apparently, Benny had been checking me out. His mamma asked my mamma, if it would be ok, if he asked me out? "Well if you could call it that?" The next thing you know, Benny would come over every Friday and my mamma would pick him up and bring him to the house with mamma, daddy, James, Kyzelle and me. Once, when we were in the car with my mamma driving, Benny touched me. He put his hand under my skirt and touched my privates. I felt so hot and wet. I liked it! Every time mamma took Benny home he touched my private spot. It felt so good. I just knew Benny and I were going to get married. We planned a double wedding with my best friend Bettina. "Well one day when we grew up."

One time Bette and I were watching cable and we saw these women that called themselves lesbians. We had no idea of what a lesbian was but they seemed like they loved each other and they were very pretty. I decided to pull a trick on Bettina. I was going to pretend to be a lesbian and pretend to like her. Bette's mother was planning a trip to New Jersey and I kept telling her that when her mother left we were going to get it on and I would wink at her. Two weeks went by, and finally it was the day that Bette's mom was leaving. When her mother slammed the door, I cornered her. Bette had the look of fear in her eyes. She said, "Lets watch TV" So we laid on the bed together and began touching each other. Bette then jumped up and ran to the bathroom and locked the door. She began crying and screaming and called me a freak. She just kept screaming, "I am not like that Fari. I am not like that!" I was so scared that I started to cry. I said, "both Bette and was sorry." I would never do that again. I told her "I was just kidding," but in my heart I knew I had feelings for her. I never thought that I was one of those lesbians? I had a boyfriend. We had plans of getting married and having children. Lesbians don't do that they just have lots of sex and smoke cigarettes right?

After that day, Bette and I drifted from best friends planning our marriages and our pregnancies together to distant strangers. I still think about Bette to this day and I wish that I could take that day back and just be best friends again. I have not seen Bettina now in about seven years and I wonder about her sometimes. I wonder did she make my life to be what it is today? Is she the reason that I became a lesbian? Or was I born this way? I remember when we met in high school, I used to tell her everyday that she looks like a doll but she would get angry and walk away. I guess my southern accent made it seem like I was saying something else. One day, Bette threw me up against the lockers and said "I DO NOT LOOK LIKE A DOG!" I chuckled and said, "doll baby doll." We were friends till the end after that day so I thought. I miss Bette so much and I hope one day she can accept me as a lesbian and understand that I just wanted to love her and be loved. But back then, I didn't understand the fear she had of me, and that God awful word that I some how grew to be, L-E-S-B-I-A-N. "Man, I hate that word." I decided that I was a choosbian. I knew that I had chose women. I could un choose them at anytime. Boys were ok but women were soft, pretty and sexy. Boys were little horn dogs that wanted to get in your panties all the time and then call you horrible names. Choosbian is what I decided to be for the rest of my life.

A few months after my seventeenth birthday, my parents gave me the worst belated birthday graduation gift ever. I got this horrible car that my father bought from the auto auction. The car had no seats or a steering wheel. It was extra old and rusty. I thought life couldn't get any worse with my two hundred dollar nightmare? But of course it did! Anyway, I didn't care about that stupid car or my graduation. My mother and father broke the worst news ever to me. We were moving from Virginia Beach to Florida. I remember my last day in Virginia and it was awful. I was crying my eyes out and clinging on to my future husband Benny. Benny was nineteen, and although I was only seventeen, I knew he was the man for me. My final memories of Virginia were sadness, hurt and just thinking my parents were worst than the devil. I knew, I would never forgive my parents for ripping me away from my future husband, my best friend and the only world I knew. I was afraid, torn and scared. Maybe I was a little excited, because Florida was supposed to be sun and fun right? Well, I hope? Once we reached Florida, my first thoughts were that I had died and gone straight to hell! I remember pulling into town and saw nothing but cows, flying roaches, lizards that ran across your feet and spiders as big as my hand. We arrived late in the evening on one of the darkest roads, I had ever seen.

The next morning, after spending the night at my mother's friend house. She was a religious fanatic. I had to sleep in the room with the filthiest girl on the planet. Justice and her farting snoring dog Harry. After a month of living with these fools and nasty girl, finally mom and dad found a house for us to live in. Then I got the bad news, we were moving to a retirement community. I knew at this point my life was pretty much over and that I would die in Florida. No Bettina, No Benny and no friends. I was doomed. I cried for what seemed like fifty days and fifty nights. Even the music in Florida sucked. I hated that boom boom booty shaking music and I hated the slow talking country folk as well. Every day for at least a year, I prayed that my parents would let me move back to Virginia to live with Bettina but mom wasn't having it. A year and a half went by in Florida and life got better. I had a new job, a car and a new identity. Back in Virginia, I was the shy little dark girl with the nappy hair, big glasses, not many friends and skinny as a rail. I was also riddled with the whole light skinned dark skinned issues stemming from Virginia. I rarely was spoken too. Any girl darker than a paper bag was considered ugly and not worthy of any respect or even acknowledgement. In Virginia, all I knew was Benny, Bettina, church and school.

BLACK LIKE ME

Safari Ann Jones

Do you want to be black like me? Long legs nappy hair black as I can be? She was born beautiful raised ugly and called nasty names and taught nasty games. Black like me nah you don't wanna be black like me. Too black, too happy darker than a paper bag. Broke as hell destined for jail and a failure in society. You wanna buy my lips my hips and learn my lingo then follow me around a store like a low life criminal? Is that all you want to be? Black girl equals nothing in this society. Invisible is what you are. When you speak no one listens your sounds are never heard. Black like me is where you want to be? As a baby my grandmothers would rock me in their arms like a precious jewel, kiss me and love me and teach me the proper way to pray. Our father who art in heaven hallowed be thy name. Can you hear me? I am silently screaming down here. Sometimes my knees get worn out trying to make it every single day. The only way I struggle through is knowing my grandmothers in heaven are holding me tight in their arms every day overseeing my blackness and making it alright when it is all wrong. Black-like-me? Are you sure that is what you want to be? The drumbeat of the Baptist church in my heart and the screams of my ancestors trapped on a slave ship destined for doom while wrapped in black. Tears flowing knowing Africa would never take them back. Everyday I am reminded that I am, my ancestors. I see I will always be Black like me. Black like me BLACK-LIKE- ME! Fade to black.

SILENT HEART

Safari Ann Jones

Sometimes my heart hurts so badly.

I cry great tears and feel so sad.

My heart is so lonely and my mind is so lame

Then why do I feel like I am ashamed?

Ashamed of my true self,

Afraid of taboo,

Hoping the real me won't really shine through.

I feel like a misfit alone in this world.

Wanting sweet love from a boy or a girl.

Not a child or a puppy I want to tame.

Just to hold my head high and sing out my name.

Sometimes my heart hurts so badly.

But my soul keeps me warm.

And my mind keeps me sad.

CHAPTER II

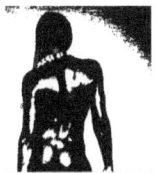

CHOCOLATE JOURNEY...

By Rose Sutra

Abused by the system, now she's shattered glass, damaged goods her life ended up in black garbage bags, hanging out with Florida hoods and jailhouse crooks...

This was her **chocolate journey**, she told me, with lips sweet, sugar chocolate kisses, wrapped in love...

Massage as we do feet together, lay side by side, I on top of her, she on top of me.

We make mad passionate luv endlessly, she says lick me, I proceed to electrocute her, the split in-between her clit, the wave that makes her body ripple flip, quiver deep within.

I say, "Can I be yours forever?"

She whispers into my left ear, "forever, ever!"

But, forever have its ups and downs are you ready to take this ride, you and me?

So we make it official, I'm hers, she's mine, our two spirits are entwining like a love spell binding.

We both look deep into each other's eyes and utter the words, "I love you."

She bits her lips, I bit mine too, we're like two erotic hot leather whips.

To be lesbian and amore her, to be woman and she love me.

She told me she would not cheat, and I believe her.

I told her I would not cheat; my only midnight creep would be with you.

We both have been hurt, cheated on and of course dating.

As I gaze into her eyes, I bit my lips aw!

This was her **chocolate journey**, sex in parked cars, parties every night, nothing she takes seriously.

She tells me life is a blast.

She finally got hired for a decent job.

Does she take anything serious?

I tell her everyday that I love her, does she believe me, or is she caught up in her latest hair weave, or in them high heal shoes she sport see?

A different pair for everyday, when will I wake up to her **chocolate journey** game?

PARTIES-N-BULLSHIT

By, Rose Sutra

I am now age nineteen, a cutie, body of life, college student, still living at
home, driving my own car, and pursuing my dream to become a rap star. I
chased my rap star dream forever. I signed four different recording
contracts and several different management contracts. I never finished
college, because of my music dream. When I look back, I don't regret
anything. I met so many great women and men along my path. I had a
blast and learned a lot. My first rap partner was a trip, but I really learned
how to flow from her. Thank you Tiesha. At the time, Tiesha did most of
the writing for the group. Tieasha did not care if I was bisexual, as long as
I did not come on to her. Back then, I was very girly. I never came on to
Tiesha. But, I did think that she was attractive and dressed really nice. We
respected one another as friends and rap partners. I met her while working
for the Attorney General's Office in Manhattan New York as Mail
Messenger Clerk. I started hanging with her after work, spending nights at
her house in the Boggie Down Bronx, and rehearsing for one entire year.
We singed three recording contracts together. The third contract at the
time would have been with Tommy Boy Records, owned at the time by
Tom Silverman. Two Shades of Black, was the name of our rap group. We
as a group gave Queen Latifah her big break. Two Shades Of Black won
that record deal contest. Queen Latifah came in second place. Tiesha did

not want to sign with Tommy Boy Records. So I followed her lead. Dam, Why did we make that dumb ass decision? But as usual back then we had got jerked. Tiesha went into the Army National Guard, graduated, went to college, got married, and birthed children. I have not seen her since. I continued pursuing music, partied and bull shitted. At the time, Hip Hop was all I wanted.

I was twenty now, stupid acting and naïve. Not taking each opportunity when given to me was a waste. The music industry parties were off the chain. I never slept with anyone in the music industry to get a record deal. Maybe that was one of my downfalls? But, in the 1980's lesbians were in the closet. Yet, I continued to go to school, work on and off. My girlfriends always took care of me while I used my money to pay for my studio recordings. I guess sex for me was equated as love. So every woman that I had sex with, I told them that I loved them. I thought it really was love. And any girl that strapped on and banged me in my ass, I went coo-coo for! But, now I know different.

I began to date other women more so at the age of 22. That is when I decided to choose women over men. I finally had chosen to be a lesbian for all that it was worth. My first as you know was Noël. She helped me to come out. But, it was when I was at my ex-lover's house that I had gone out with this Jamaican guy named Derrick that told me he would buy me a

Mercedes Benz, if I had sex with him. I wasn't with Genie long, so I said to myself, "What the hell?" Derrick had called me up that day and asked if I wanted to hang out with him. I told him I would. When he came to pick me up, we drove to a hotel in Queens New York. He paid for the room. While we were in the room, we started having sex. There was no foreplay. He just wanted to stick it in. When he had pulled out his penis, my face dropped! I had never in my life seen a penis that big. It looked like something that belonged to a big gorilla! He proceeded many times to try to stick his horse dick into my deer vagina. Since it would not fit in the front, I suggested my ass! He said, "No that was nasty." It was not happening, and at this point, I knew, I would not be getting my Mercedes Benz. I got up and went to the bathroom to get dressed. I came out of the bathroom and told him, "Can you please drive me back to my girlfriends house." He said, "Ok."

When I returned to Genie's house, she opened the door and said, "Where did you go?" I did not give her and answer. I headed to the bathroom, to take a shower and brush my teeth. After I had taken a shower, I proceeded to reach down to pick up my toothbrush, when I chipped my front tooth on the bathroom sink. To this day, I still have that chipped tooth. It was at this point in my life that I had stopped dating men. I had made my choice. I was a lesbian for life.

It was now the year 1993, my mother Doreen, my father Jason, and my Sister Lorilie passed away one month after each other. My mother was a functioning drug attic that worked as a drug counselor for ST. Mary's hospital in Brooklyn New York. My mother had died in the hospital in Queens New York. I don't know what she died from. She had just come out of the hospital and she was feeling well. I had received a phone call from my father two-weeks later, telling me that my mother had died. Why didn't he call me when she was in the hospital? My mother did give me a phone call and had said days before she died, "Your father is abusing me." I really got tired of him hitting on her. I asked her to come stay with me, but she told me no. I guess at this point, she liked being abused. I could no longer jump into their fights and try to stop it. I listened to my mother and begged her once again to leave him. We hung up the phone. I had said to myself, "God take her life, because I can't help her anymore." I know that was mean to think and pray, but my father had abused her from day one. I never attended my mother's funeral. Why? I would have killed my Father on the day of the funeral. I chose not to attend. After my second mother died, that's when I chose to stop rapping and write poetry.

My Uncle whom I referred to as my father was a veteran of WWII. He was a functioning drug attic, and hustler that worked as a cook for Newsweek Magazine in New York City. My mother was a functioning drug attic that worked as a drug counselor for ST. Mary's hospital in

Brooklyn New York. My Sister worked was a Secretary for IBM in New York City. My sister, brother and I never wanted for anything. My parents owned a house in Cambria Heights, Queens New York. My Sister lived in the Bronx. I grew up as a child jumping into my mother and fathers fights always trying to protect her. To this day I am over protective of women that are very close to me.

August 1993, my Father passed away. I attended his funeral to make sure he was dead. Dead for all the times he hit and bruised my mother's body. Dead for all the times he patted me on my ass. Dead for that one time he tried to come on to me. That Mother Fucker was six deep under and I was happy. At this point, I hated him, and anything that a man stood for. I was really a lesbian for life now.

September 1993, my sister had passed away. Lorilie was heavy on drugs. She died from HIV Aids. She simply fell apart after my mother had died. I always tried to call and check up on her, but she avoided me. Until one day, I was out vending my poetry cd's on Parson's and Archer in Queens New York. I looked across the street and I saw my Sister. I said to myself, "There goes my Sister," I started waving. I was getting ready to run across the street, when she disappeared. I thought to myself that was weird. I had left the avenue and went home. I had received a phone call from my aunt Joyce that night telling me that my Sister died last night. I thought to myself "Was that her astral body traveling and saying good-bye to me?" I attended her funeral. I did not get to see her body. From what my aunt Joyce told me. She was skin and bones. The drugs and HIV Aids ate her up.

ROSE 25

One year has passed, and I'm twenty-five years old now. I enrolled myself back in to college. I continued on my path of music. But, now I decided to be a poet. I started hanging out on the poetry scene. I ran with mad poets. I studied styles of poet's performances and lyrics for about six months. I hung out at The Brooklyn Moon Café' every Friday night, the African Poetry Theater, Nu York Rican Poet's Café', Jimmy's Uptown Café', The Apollo, and several other spots. I admired Israel Tacoma, Bruce George, Nikki Giovanni, Malcolm X, Martin Luther King, Tantra, Blue, Shariff Simmons, and so many others. I wrote several strong poetry pieces after my parents and sister had died. My poetry was conscious, radical, hard core, sweet and sincere most of the time. I very rarely wrote about love. At this point, I did not know what love was anymore. For me it was all about anger and revenge. You name it I was down with it. I went in and out of town with women, not finishing my education, and not dedicating the time to my music. I literally fell into the trap called, "The Life!" I lived, breathed, tasted and loved it. At the time, I could not see past the club, the fems, the dykes or the strap-on dildos. I was lost. I think after my moms and sister died, I wanted to be lost. So, I started hanging out at Gay clubs, having one-nightstands, getting drunk and high. But I never gave up writing poetry. My experiences drove me to create some great poetry pieces.

PARTIES-N-BULLSHIT

By, Safari

Sometmes, I sit and think of all the parties and wild club scenes I have
been in. On the gay scene parties and drugs sometimes go hand and hand.
Don't get me wrong because there are clean and sober lesbians out there.
The problem is that most lesbians are under so much pressure to fit in this
world of fire and brimstone and self-righteous straightness. A lot lesbian's
have emotional issues. I can only speak from my experiences with lesbians
I have encountered. I have encountered some women with terrible mental
issues that stem from family life, rape, bad relationships and heartaches
caused by women and men. Honestly, being a lesbian of color is like being
any other woman of color but to the third power. Some people call us
triple threats. Being black, female and lesbian sometimes adds to the
pressure of life because we are discriminated against in society, church
and the gay community. Most of the time we feel invisible and under
represented. Most would say black and gay? No way, but I say oh yes, we
are here and we aint goin nowhere. I think that lesbians of color are a great
anomaly of nature because how interesting is it that it takes two straight
people to make us? So, I guess two gay people would make a straight kid
right?

Well back to the parties and bullshit. I grew up around all kinds of partying and drinking as a kid. My father was a Navy man so all my life, I remember the fantastic military parties and family events that we attended all the time. Those parties impacted my life because as my parents and their friends danced and drank the night away. So did I. I was three years old the first time I had got drunk. I remember it was my brother James's idea and my big brother to me was a genius for five years old. He was the leader and I was a follower. My sister Kyzelle was always my protector and she kept her eyes open for the antics of James and I. Kyzelle knew that James and I had a knack for getting into things and she was mama's eagle eyes. That ruined a lot of our fun and helped deliver a lot of spankins but heck that didn't stop the dynamic two-oh! One time, my parents had this huge birthday party and mama put James and I to bed and off she went to enjoy the festivities. Mama was known for her fabulous cooking, scrumptious barbeque sauce. Mama was the champion of cooking and the best party giver in town. I remember mama used to make so many yummy goodies. My favorites were the turkey, cheese, pepperoni, and olives on a toothpick. James and I would steal them from the table during our stakeout. I was sure mama was super mama in an apron because she was on top of everything all night. Mama barely drank anything daddy was quite the lush. Daddy lived to party and drink and I guess that tradition was not mama's thing. The liquor bottle was one of daddy's best friends and all of daddy's military friends lived for a good party. I hated that even then because neither daddy nor his friends ever helped mama with anything but they would eat and be merry and go to bed drunker than a skunk and daddy's friends would leave mama alone and exhausted. I vowed that I would never grow up and marry a man because to me mama was a house slave and I wanted to travel the world not clean the house all my life. Mama would pass out from exhaustion after every party but not till she cleaned the entire house and checked on James and I. Normally, we were tucked away in our beds dreaming of monsters and lollypops. Mama always checked on us at least three times to make sure we were sleeping. James and I would pretend to be sleeping and would sneak downstairs then crawl behind the sectional sofa like we were in war ducking from flying shrapnel. While hidden behind the sofa we would sneak food and sip all of the adult drinks. I was only three so I didn't know what adult drinks were but I knew drinking them were bad for children. I figured since James was a genius and all that it would be ok. We maneuvered oh so carefully because I knew if mama ever caught us we were in for a serious butt whoopin. James was always the smartest big brother in the world and he was my hero. So like the swat team going in for the sting we skillfully moved in on our party kill. We crawled, ducked and stayed low. James began our ritualistic adult drink sipping game. He would reach his hand up to the end tables and grab an adult drink and we would both take a sip and then put it back. Adult drinks sometimes tasted like candy but some of them tasted like varnish and juice. I liked the way the adult drinks would make us giggle and feel funny, just like the adults. At the end of the night, mama and her friends were on the hunt for James and Fari whom mama referred to as her bad butt twins. Kyzelle screamed out "maaaaaaaamaaaaaaaaaaaaa" I found Fari and she stinks." Ky had seen my pink little elephant foot in jimmies sticking out and dragged me from behind that couch. Mama came closer to inspect James and I and exclaimed, " These two fools are drunk". The next day, I was sure we were going to get a spankin but mama just lectured us about adult drinks. She told us never drink adult drinks even when you are an adult because they will make you crazy, have bad spirits and make you sick. That day, I decided that adult drinks were not for me. I decided that I didn't want to be any part of bad spirits, being sick and crazy. I promised mama that I would never touch adult drinks again. I wish I could've lived up to that promise.

As, I went into my teen years I didn't drink alcohol but I loved to dance and party. I couldn't wait to turn twenty-one and be legal so I could hang out with all my friends in the nightclubs. Dancing was my life. It gave me freedom and way to express myself. One night while in the club, I met this really tall guy. I was wearing my brand new daisy duke shorts and he tried to get my attention by grabbing one of my back pockets but his hand slid down and caught one of my ruffles that went around the cheek of my behind. It ripped my ruffle half was off my shorts and boy was I pissed. I

41

didn't want any part of this fresh young man with no manners. I told this fellow off and walked away. I assumed he played basketball or something but I didn't care about that. Most of the girls would've seen his height and threw themselves at this giant of darkness but I walked away with an attitude never looking back. Weeks later, I was at another local nightclub and I saw this same tall and goofy guy dancing like a total doofball. I swear this guy had to be about twenty feet tall and doing the hammer and the running man. Kyzelle was with me and we just stared at this fool because he looked crazy but he kept smiling and dancing and didn't care who stared at him. I found out weeks later, that this dancing fool was named Shaquille O'Neil. I had no clue of who this guy was but I started to see him on television shows and I heard he couldn't shoot a three pointer to save his life. My chance meeting with Shaquille became the story of my life. I for some reason met several celebrities throughout my life and none of them seemed to really change or impact my life. I sometimes wonder could Shaquille have been the husband that was intended for me or is this gay mixed up world where I belong? I guess, I will never know and that multimillion-dollar doofball won't know either. I like Shaq, but I really think hammer pants are not his thing.

LIQUID SANITY?

What does my liquid sanity mean to me? Smiling dancing positivity. Life is so hard and full of anguish and frustration. Yet, liquid sanity is your only form of communication. Liquid sanity? Is it really sanity in a bottle? Or is it trouble, pain a horror movie speeding at full throttle in a bottle? Liquid sanity is what you make it. It is a form of courage when you have none, a stress reliever when you need some. A way to take away the pain or is it an express ride to hell? Is liquid sanity the road to insanity? Demons and spirits possessing my soul and making me prance in a liquid prance as I dance in the liquid. As I sip my insanity away, I step into the sane dream world of liquid insanity. Doctor can you help me?

DANCE WITH THE LIQUID DEVIL

By Safari

In my early twenties drinking was introduced to me by a girlfriend. She had a high profile job and a high tolerance for alcohol and weed. I learned a lot from this lost soul. I learned what not to do for the rest of my life. I would pay the price of my lessons learned. She taught me to drink alcohol for breakfast, lunch and dinner. We used to have Mimosa's for breakfast, Martini's for lunch and champagne and wine for dinner. My life became a drunken stupor. Drinking started out being fun and exciting but later on my health started to deteriorate. I became lost in the pits of alcoholism. Alcohol became my best friend, lover, mother, comfort and worst enemy all rolled into one. Life in the lesbian world has assisted in the acceleration of my alcoholism. I have hit rock bottom several times and have spent many nights on dirty bathroom floors. I wonder how a sweet smart little church girl from Ohio became a lost, lesbian alcoholic? The lesbian community can take a toll on a person. Most of the time I have spent in bad relationships being abused by women. I have been used for my looks, money or time. Dating women for me has been a tragedy, comedy and horror movie wrapped into an exciting yet heartbreaking life. I have spent a majority of my young life on the gay scene. There are a lot of drug addicts and alcoholics in the gay world, just like the straight world. The gay and straight world shares the same wicked addictions and in both worlds they are equally as lethal. Most people in the gay community use drugs and alcohol to numb the pain of having to hide in fear and others use them as a stress reliever. I can recall once as a teenager, I was hanging out in an all night rave club and I saw at least three to five drug overdoses in one night. One girl was in the bathroom slobbering as her friends fed her sugar. I remember thinking these straight white kids are crazy. Once I hung out with a friend and bartender friend of mine Maurine. Maurine and I went to a nice Italian dinner and then off to the club we went. All night we drank wine. I woke up the next morning between two naked women. One was Maurine and the other was a friend of hers. I was terrified that I had blacked out from all the drinking. "What had I done?" I asked Maureen what happened and she said, "You don't remember Fari?" I said, " Well, uh no." Maurine looked at me puzzled and said we had a foursome. I yelled "WHAT?" Maurine and her friend began to laugh and as they were laughing a naked guy got up from the floor. I was not laughing but eventually I realized the joke was on me. I knew then that alcohol could be lethal. I should've known, because Maureen was straight. But when you drink alcohol you sometimes wake up in some of the strangest places!

One night, I met a married straight couple at a gay club. I thought, "Hhell I am single and cant find a decent woman so I could do a little experimenting to test the waters of my gayness." I slept with the couple but I refused to let the man penetrate me or come to close to me. The wife I wasn't fond of and despite the kissing and rubbing and watching them have sex, I stood on the sidelines. We were stone cold drunk, but I held strong to my lesbianism. Most of that night was a total blurr. The next day, they called me and I told them that I could never be with them again. The threesome thing was just not for me. I didn't understand why I was trying to conform to societies standard of right or wrong when it came to sexuality. I think sometimes that the years of brainwashing in the black church corrupted my mind and confused my morals. All those years of praying got me here. The hardest thing about being a gay black woman is that most of us fear being cast out from out communities and families. The black culture consists of our family and church, as being our base so to lose that would be an awful tragedy to bear alone. Most of us hide because we are under the rule of the BLACK CHURCH!! The black church is a falsely loving environment and an unforgiving place to gay people. Fire and brimstone and the pits of hell are seared into a gay persons heart and mind so much that we sometimes fear ourselves. Guilt and shame usually follow then comes alcohol and some cases drugs. Not all lesbians out their experience the drug and alcohol issues but social acceptance in the black community and church are still an issue to this day. Most gay blacks now attend gay churches. Gay churches are so nice because it feels so good to be able to worship God with the friends and family who love you for who you are. It just feels good to be free to just be comfortable holding your girlfriend's hand in prayer. I think if a lot of the straight world knew gay churches existed they would dowse the church and all the members with gasoline and burn the churches to the ground in the name of the Lord. Bible thumping extremist can be funny like that sometimes. The black church is sometimes one of the most unforgiving places that a child can be raised in. I was raised in the black church all of my life, until I was in my early twenties. Church was my backbone, my structure, and my life. Most of my teenage years were spent in the church praying for miracles and clapping to the thunderous drumbeats of the choir's drummer. I have always adored church and I had so much respect for our pastor and the churches elders. I came from a long line of praying grandmothers, grandfathers and love for the church. Family has always filled my heart. Church was always a source of spirituality and a way to socialize. The Baptist church should be made into a miniseries because within it is drama, comedy, racism and a whole lot of gossip. I think I acquired my great communication skills from all the church gossip. Church played a huge part in shaping my life good and bad. To me church was like a Sunday triathlon. We were in church from 7PM. till about 8PM. throughout the week we rehearsed our songs for the choir, usher board and any other activities. When you are a Baptist you spend your life at church so it influences you to think act and live your life as a Baptist. Anything out of the church standards is considered taboo. The Baptist church to me is like a double-edged sword. Everything is considered a sin, yet if you

47

watch and listen you will see and hear all kinds of sins being committed. As a teenager, the Baptist idea of being Godly and perfect was constantly being imposed on us. Eventually, I realized that the black church used the bible as a weapon. The bible was always used as a way to control the minds of the masses. To this day, I still crack up knowing that the black churches used to abide by the rules of the King James bible but I am sure most of the members would collapse in shock to find out King James was a gay man with many lovers. In church, I witnessed a lot of horrific and shocking things. Once, when I was about fourteen a friend of mine named Terrie was alone in the baptism tub area of the church and something bad happened to her. Terrie's mom was looking for her because it was almost time for our bible study lesson. Mrs. Page said "Safari have you seen Terrie?" I said, "Yes maam, she went to the ladies room because she lost her sweater and thought maybe she left it in there." Mrs. Page asked me and Grace to look for Terrie, so we wouldn't be late to our lesson. Our church was huge so we needed all the help we could get. We searched all over the church and finally I went in the baptism room. To my astonishment, Terrie was laying on the floor with her skirt up and her panties down to her ankles. She looked like she was either sleeping or dead. I screamed and I ran. A few days later, I overheard mama and the gossiping ladies of the church talking about Terrie. My grandma used to call the gossiping ladies of the church hens. The hens were cackling and I overheard one of them say Terrie had been raped and sodomized.

Somehow she was knocked unconscious and when she came to she was crazier than a loon. After the Terrie incident my mama maintained her eagle eyes and watched me like a hawk. I know it was just form my protection because she loved me dearly and wouldn't ever want to see me hurt.

The teenagers of the church used to steal away from our parents and play nasty games and gossip. Our favorite thing was to hide from the adults and ditch that boring long sermon. We all hate church sermons. They were the longest drawn out stories of the bible. As teenagers, we always tried to escape as much as possible. One day, we were in our favorite spot called the cry room. This room was made for those with babies who were crying so that the parents could enjoy the church service and not disturb others. This booth was sound proof so it was perfect for talking and playing around. We were having a hell of a time when the notorious teen stalker, head deaconess, of the church Mrs. Spellz the tattletale came a huntin. The cry room had a huge clear Plexiglas window and a speaker that you could turn off when you wanted silence. The room was positioned in the very back of the church so it was a perfect hide out. I was smart enough to realized that most of our mama's were on the usher board so the patrolled the church like the FBI. I realized that when you sit in the far right corner of the cry room no one in the congregation could see you because it was blind spot. All of a sudden, the entire congregation turned around and all you saw were mothers and fathers moving their heads up and down and side to side trying to see who was in the cry room. None of the other teens saw what was going on, so I opened the door and dropped to my hands and knees and crawled out the door as fast as I could. My friend Nannette saw me and did the same. The other kids were having so much fun laughing and playing that they still didn't notice the doom was coming. Nanette and I knew the escape drill because we practiced our escape many times and this time it came in handy. One of the worst things that you can do if you have a black mama is to be disobedient and to embarrass her at church and make her the gossip topic of the week. If you crossed that line you knew you were guaranteed a major butt whoopin in front of your friends and the entire congregation would hear you screaming. Nannette and I ran for the ladies lounge and then into the bathroom stalls. We knew Mrs. Spellz was coming to sniff us out. I was so scared, because I knew mama would try to kill me if she knew I was with the other kids fooling around in church. Nanette and I locked the stall doors and stood up on the top of the toilets to hide our feet. I held my breath praying Mrs. Spellz wouldn't sniff us out. I could hear her bright white stalker nurse shoes squeaking towards my fate. She stopped peeked under the doors for feet and screeched out" Ladies if you are in hear come out now!! If you know what's good for ya. I began to swear but I wasn't giving myself up. I felt like game waiting to be hunted and killed. As I closed my eyes and prayed the raid suddenly came to a halt. Old lady Klein and her grand daughter

Kia came into the bathroom. Mrs. Spellz forgot that she was stalking us teens and began to gossip about the pastor and his wife and kids. Kia began to prance around and say "Mamah pee pee now! Right now! Mrs. Spellz excused herself and said "Take that baby to the bathroom chile" I breathed a sigh of relief. I didn't move because I knew if Kia spotted me, my cover would be blown. Kia was only two but she knew my face. All of a sudden, Kia peeked her head under the stall door and said " faaaaaa faaaaa Mamah faaaaa faaaaaa baaaathoooom. Nanette must've sensed that I was in a jam so she pulled out a tiny lollypop and shoved it out of the stall and Kia followed it. Soon old lady Klein grabbed Kia by the hand not noticing her new lollipop and left. Our reign of terror was finally over.

In church there was always organized racism that no one ever realized or recognized. The pastor of our church always referred to white people as white fok and would warn us to be on our best behavior when the white folk were around. I always wondered why we had to behave around white folk. Why couldn't we just be ourselves? I mean was there a rule somewhere that said that we are not allowed to be ourselves? This strange phenomenon baffled me for years. I can still hear my mother saying "Shhhhush yall and quit actin a fool! White folk already think we are crazy". I will never understand the rule of the white folk because as far as I can see they are just as crazy as we are. Gay people were the unspoken taboo. Our pastor's very own son Torrence showed the very gay trait that his father preached against. Torrence was swishy and very effeminate and had many friends that were just like he was. I swear Torrence and his swishy boyfriends could out play a tambourine better than any woman I have ever seen. I used to think that they should have the tambourine Olympics, when I watched Torrence play it. I recall seeing so many gay men in church but no one ever spoke of the gayness. I do recall my mama and the hens gossiping about the sissy boys and how prissy and prim the would play the tambourine or how they would march down the isle with the choir with the swishy swish in their hips. Once a cross-dresser man come to our church. He was a pianist for a visiting choir. This person had on a woman's shirt, a wig and a woman's blouse. Under his robe he had on women's pants and men's shoes! This was the talk of the town. During the after church dinner the hens were cackling and I heard "Chile did you see that man thang playin the piano?" "Girl yeah, what was that anyway?" Then the all laughed hysterically. Somebody then said, "Them sissy boys should be ashamed of themselves parading around this church." Don't they know they are going straight to hell?" "God don't like no homosexuals and they are truly hell bound." I then heard an echo of "Amens" and "Thank ya Jesus." One lady even said, "The pastor shouldn't allow those heathens in our church corrupting our children." I do recall my mama as always being the liberal one. She would giggle with the rest of the hens but I do remember her always having gay friends. When I was about three years old, I remember a man that was always in the beauty salon. His name was Pretty Wayne. Pretty Wayne was always dressed like a gay pimp. Wayne would wear loud colors like yellow, red pink or electric blue suits. He had long women's fingernails and always wore a wide brimmed hat and long Shirley Temple curls with matching women's heels. Pretty Wayne was always dressed to kill and I was crazy about him. Pretty Wayne was so clean and sharp looking and very feminine, but I never thought much about the feminine side of him. I always thought Pretty Wayne looked like Super fly and a cool pimp. He was always so nice, sweet, stylish and so gay. At three years old, I didn't know what gay is and really didn't care. All I knew is that I wanted to grow up to be pretty just like Pretty Wayne. My mother had another friend that I presumed was gay, as well. His name was Jerry and he was a drag queen. By day, Jerry was a chef and at night he was a drag queen. Jerry worked with mama at the military base's chow all. Jerry had the best-plucked eyebrows in town. He had all kinds of wigs, gowns and photos of him dressing as a woman. I was at least twelve years old around this time, so I was aware that something was up with Jerry. My mom used to love to swap beauty secrets with Jerry. Heck, gay men and drag queens seem to have the best makeup tips; well at least that is what my mama always said. I don't remember ever thinking too much of Jerry's gayness and mama never said too much of anything about it. Gay has always been the unspoken wicked and evil thing that no one acknowledged, so it didn't exist. Did it? In the black community if something is taboo and unspoken then it doesn't exist and superstition is like the gospel directly from God. If the pastor in church said it then it must be so. I call it black washing. Early on in my life I learnt to be gay or what I call a choosbian is to be hushed and non-existent. Hiding and lying about who I am, is a must and inevitable. Knowing this fact shaped my mental health and my future in the lesbian world. I was in for a rude awakening yet like a sacrificial baby my innocence and naivety was about to be ripped out of my body and stomped like a homosexual in Jamaica! The lessons were coming and I wasn't ready for battle just yet.

THE HOUND-SAFARI

The Hound was a friend of my brother James. He got his name from his style of rap that he did. The Hound was of island decent and his rap style was laid back but fierce. His lyrics were so deep. I used to stare at him as he laid down his raps. His Caribbean heritage helped him flip flop his rap style to another level of funk mixed with island slang. The Hounds lyrics would take you on a journey and back again. I loved his style and I knew some day he would be a star. The Hound was a rapper and a kind and very sweet guy. I used to talk to him all the time in my parents garage. James had turned our old dirty garage into a recording studio where all the local rappers came to rehearse before they went to the studio. I really liked the Hound and secretly thought he was kinda cute. I used to talk to the Hound all the time and he was really going through some bad things. One day while sitting in the studio he started talking to me about his life. I asked him why he was so sad and he explained to me that he was about to go on trial for attempted murder and accessory to a crime. He and his two friends Chris and Rayvon were downtown Orlando and got into a world of trouble. Rayvon was anxious to brandish and use his new gun on something or somebody. A couple was walking down the street when Rayvon decided that he would rob them. For no real reason at all Rayvon shot the woman in the face. It turns out that she and her boyfriend were celebrating a special occasion together and their celebration turned into a helluva night. All the boys ran for cover and The Hood told me that they tried all night to stop waxing that gun and behaving foolishly. Of course Rayvon didn't listen and now all of their natural lives were in danger because of Rayvon's actions they would probably spend the rest of their lives in prison. The Hound showed me his electronic ankle bracelet courtesy of the Orlando police department thanks to Rayvon. He told me he was trying to turn his life around and was regularly attending church. He was hoping that the jury would spare him since this was his first offense. I assured him that everything would be ok. I told him to stay positive, pray and stay out of trouble. One night, my current girlfriend and I went to a local sandwich shop and The Hound was there working. I was so happy to see him prospering. He seemed a little glum and serious no smiles and no happiness in his face. I wondered what was wrong because he smiled all the time and his heart always seemed like it was on the brink of happiness. On this day, I didn't see a sign of any of the invariance that I knew he always had. We left and I thought that maybe his trial and everything was getting to him. About three weeks later, while watching the news my brother called and sounded so upset. He told me that he just found out that The Hound was dead. He was having baby mama drama and he decided to get a gun and shoot the mother of his kids and several members of her family. Next, he killed himself. I was so sad to hear the news of the Hounds death because once again it seemed as if death and destruction was becoming part of my life and the sad part is that I was learning to accept death as something normal.

STUDIO - SAFARI

I decided to enroll in community college to further my life. Heck, I had nothing else to do? My local community college was like high school revisited. I explored every inch of my school and I embarked on a few new adventures in the process of learning, men and partying was my new thing. In Virginia I was called ugly and blacky because of my reddish clay brown skin but in Florida I was the next new hot thing. I made very good grades and had no idea of what career path I would follow. I did at least know that I would have as many dates that I could stand. In Virginia, I didn't get this luxury of men wanting little ole me. Blacky, got a date only during black history month, if I was lucky! Heck, if didn't have bad luck, I wouldn't have any luck at all! I went into date overload. I was not letting the equal opportunity pass me by. I was scared that the fun and dates would all end and I would be back in Virginia. All of the dating became very demanding on my time. I remember having four dates in one day! I had to slow it down. Eventually, I had to slow down with the dates and have a little fun. One day, I met up with this guy in my human sexuality class they called him Phats. Phats had chocolate brown skin, a low haircut and the biggest juiciest butt I have ever seen on a man. Most of the girls called him Big Booty Phats. Yep, Phats had a way with the ladies. One day Phats asked me if I wanted to chill with him and his friends. I was like well heck why not. I was so excited when Teddy told them that we were going to a real live recording studio. I acted cool, but I wanted to scream with delight. I had never been to a recording studio before. I had dreamed of being a singing star all my life. Little did I know that the trip to the studio would change my life forever? After class, Phats and I headed for the recording studio. I still can remember the entire male faces that stared my way as I walked in the sound proof room. Phats introduced me "This is Safari from my school." I was kind of shy and nervous. I gave just a little wave and a smile. This one guy in the back of the you said, "Oh so, we got us a schoolgirl in the house." He started laughing. Every since that day, I was known as schoolgirl and they were known as The Boys. The Boys protected me like I was their baby sister. I was in awe by all the gold diamonds and matching Mercedes Benz's that they all had. These dudes were rich as hell. They used to order tons of pizza's with all the toppings and I loved being around these guys because money was not object. I just knew that one day The Boys would let me sing, maybe a bit part on a record and make me a star. That day never came though. I sang around them every chance that I got, but they always thought I was just too cute and well that's about it. In my heart I knew I would be the next superstar, but no one else could hear me dreaming. I went to the studio every day for the next year right after school to hang out with the studio engineers and of course The Boys. I learned really fast that The Boys had lots of money and lots of really stupid women that they called hoochie hoes. These women would do anything with anybody just to get a chance to hang out with The Boys. I am sure glad I didn't have to be a hoochie hoe because they used to talk about those girls like dogs. I decided, that I would start my own business. One day while massaging Phat's Hands, one of The Boys offered me money for a massage. His name was Big Daddy Ching but everyone called him Ching for short. Ching was the boss of all The Boys. He was the richest, the most powerfulness, everybody looked up to him, and gave him much respect. If you didn't you would get the serious beat down. Daddy Boy had so many gold teeth that when he smiled you would swear you had went blind for a second. He wore lots of rings with big shiny diamonds and hundreds of gold chains. I had never in my life seen so many gold chains and diamonds in my life. I had never owned a diamond in my life. I daydreamed sometimes that all of Daddy Boy's diamonds were mine and I was the richest girl in the world, but the sad truth was that I was a middle class girl with stingy parents. I remember Daddy Boy paid me twenty dollars and I used to charge Phats only five bucks. That day Daddy Ching announced to everyone in the room that from now on they would all have to pay me for my massages. He said, "This little girl is going to be something special one day." She is going to be educated unlike you dumb mothafucka's." After that day, I started making extra cash from The Boys and I spent a lot of late nights massaging hands and feet. One night at the studio Daddy Boy, Phats and I sat in the lobby of the studio and Daddy Boy was imitating Phats. Phats had entered and won booty shake contest. Daddy Boy was determined that he was going to describe the whole scenario to me. According to Daddy Boy, Phats had on bikini leopard print underwear and was shaking his booty like a jelly bowl. We were all cracking up at he was telling the story and Daddy Boy jumped on top of the table and started doing the Big Booty Phats dance Ching looked at his watch and said "School girl it is kind of late girl." It is time for you to go home and get your homework done. "Now get girl before I have to take my belt off and call Phats when you get home." Phats walked me to the car and kissed my cheek goodnight like he always had and he watched me drive out of the parking lot. The next week was so stressful and I noticed that I didn't see Phats in class all week. It was rumored that Phats was a crack fiend and may have AIDS but I wasn't sure about those rumors and I didn't care. As I was getting ready for class I saw this commercial. It was a model search here in Orlando. I begged my mamma to give me two hundred dollars so I could enter my summer job had ended and I was dead broke. Of course, mamma said, "no," as usual.

That evening, I devised a plan to get some money so I could partake in the model search. I would show my stingy old mamma and when I was famous I was going to act like I didn't know her or my stingy daddy. I called my friend Karen Latrice and told her I wanted to go to work with her. She said "Fari have you fell and bumped your head girl?" I told Karen that I knew what I was doing and that I needed money fast and if she wouldn't help me then I would work down Orange Blossom trail on my own. Karen looked at me like a little sister so she said "Ok fair just this once I will help you get out of a jam but just this once cause I don't want your mamma coming to slap me with a bible." I had no idea what I was supposed to do at this job or how to act because I had never been a prostitute before. I was about to turn my first trick and I had no clue of what was in store for me. I just prayed to God that I didn't get killed or put in jail. Karen had a regular John, named Joe. Joe was married with four grown kids and was a rich old wrinkled white man who had the littlest penis I had ever seen, and probably held the little ding a ling worlds record. Would you believe this fool didn't want to have intercourse with us? This crazy man made Karen and I dress up like cowgirls and dance in thongs, cowboy hats and boots and topless to country music. He made us dance fast then slow, fast then slow. I thought this man was a true nutcase. He would jack himself off while watching us. What a sicko. Later, Joe said, "He wanted to give me oral sex." I was scared to death, but I let him. He licked and licked and then he started chewing on my clitoris like he was chomping on a piece of gum. I was so glad when he said, "He wanted to see some girl on girl action and he asked Karen to pleasure me." I was so glad. She was so gentle and I didn't mind her tongue at all. All I could think of is getting my money and leaving. While I was staring at the ceiling trying to pretend I was not there. There was a knock at the door and I was terrified. Karen tried to assure me that everything was cool, but I just knew I was going to jail after turning my very first trick. Joe went to the door and there was skinny buggy eyed girl at the door she was begging him to let her in so she could make him feel good. He screamed for her to leave and told her don't come back and slammed the door in her face. Finally, after about two hours and for me it seemed like two years, old whitey pulled out his wallet and gave us one hundred dollars apiece. That day, I vowed to never turn a trick again because it was easy yet scary and jail didn't seem like my kind of place for one hundred bucks. So I started looking for a job the next day. I swear, I looked for a job for weeks but each job told me that because I had no prior experience that they couldn't hire me. I thought well why would a company not give a young person a chance so they could get experience? One day, I was looking at the local newspaper and I saw an ad that said they were looking for lingerie models.

I thought to myself, well I want to be a model and lingerie is very pretty so why not? It's a job right? So I called the number and man told me to meet him near a street called Gore. He told me to bring some lingerie to model. I didn't have any lingerie but I had a swimsuit, heels and a silky nightgown that my best friend bought me for graduation. I was sure this was the right job. I headed out across town to find my new job. I drove round and round trying to find this place and I ended up in this really seedy looking neighborhood. It was dirty and not very safe looking. I was sure that this was not where I was supposed to meet this man that said I could make a lot of money. I went to the nearest convenience store to call him and he said his name was Kevlove and that he was just around the corner and he would be standing in the yard waiting on me. I hopped back into my car and I drove slowly down the dark and dirty street. I looked around and I saw nothing but old dirty shacks and a scruffy dog tied to an old rusty fence. Then I saw this really dark skinned man with a big shiny gold tooth and one big gold medallion around his neck standing in the yard. He had on dress pants a colorful shirt and some really shiny shoes. I rolled down my window to yell out to him but something told me to remain silent so I just stared at him and he stared at me as he talked to someone on his huge white cell phone. It seemed that everything started to move in slow motion and I couldn't hear a sound except for my heavy breathing. I remember looking at the man to my right but to my left I saw a glimpse of some kid of commotion. I turned slowly to my left to see a black van with no windows. It pulled up right next to me. Suddenly, the sliding door on the side of the van opened up and about twenty men with black ski masks jumped out of the van and ran around my car and tackled the man in the yard. I thought about hitting the gas and getting the hell out or there as soon as possible, but I sat there cautiously awaiting their next move and planning my escape. My heart started beating so fast as I observed the masked men beating the man senseless, yelling obscenities and handcuffing him. When I realized that they were not paying attention to me, I carefully pressed the gas pedal and I drove slowly out of the neighborhood and went home. I had no idea of what I had just witnessed but whatever it was it was not a good thing. When I got home, I called Phats and told him what happened. I can still hear him screaming in the phone " WHAT" "Schoolgirl, have you lost your damn mind?" I didn't understand what I had done or why he was so upset. I was just trying to get a job and pay my way since my parents were son stingy with their money. Heck I needed some cold cash and it wasn't coming fast enough. Phats was so pissed off at me and he said, " School Girl do you realize that that man was a pimp and he and his boys were probably going to initiate you?" I said, "Initiate?" Well of course Phats told me all I had to do was model and boom I would have tons of cash. Teddy got silent and sounded like he was so angry that he could just strangle me. Teddy then yelled so loud in the phone that I had to take the phone away from my ear. "SAFARI ANN JONES THEY WERE GOING TO GANG RAPE YOU!"

I was dead silent and I couldn't believe what I had heard. It sounded like Phats looked like he was about to cry so he said, "Stay by the phone I need to take care of business." About thirty minutes later, Phats called me back and said get dressed because Ching wants to talk to you. Oh boy, I knew I was in trouble now. I couldn't believe how stupid and naive I was. I had walked into a trap, and I knew Ching was gonna let me have it. I wasn't scared of Ching, but I knew his words could make a grown man shiver. I had seen Ching beat grown men like they stole something and make them cry. When Phats pulled up, I hung my head low in pure shame. I knew I had messed up, and I was going to hear about it. In the car there was silence and as we reached the studio Phats said, "No need in giving the sad face schoolgirl and looking all innocent because Ching knows what you did and you're going to get it. I was afraid of a man for the first time in my life. I think my heart stopped, and I walked as slow as I could was hoping that I would drop dead before I faced Ching. As soon as I saw his face and his mouth full of gold the tears in my eyes stung like fire. I swear you couldn't hear a pen drop. Ching ordered everyone except me to leave the room. Ching was the boss man and had the money and the power and guns to prove it and they all knew it and gave him much respect. His words were like the words of Jesus and they boys were his disciples. I felt like the sacrificial lamb about to be slaughtered. Through my tears, I saw big boy stand up and take off his leather belt. He put his gun on the table. I shook with so much fear. I was afraid to take a breath. Big Boy lunged at me and snatched me up in my collar and slammed my back up against the wall. I knew he was either going to kill me or beat me to death. Ching. proceeded to hit me with the leather belt over and over, until I started screaming and fell to the floor. Phats ran in the room, and yelled out "Man stop you are going to kill her." I knew Phats must've had a moment of insanity or he really cared about me, because no fool would talk to Ching like that. Big Boy picked me up from the floor. He threw me in the chair. He was breathing so hard. I was crying like a little baby. Ching walked out of the room and slammed the door. Ching came back about five minutes late, and said, "Schoolgirl what the hell were u thinking?" All I could utter through the crying was "I model, money no money, I am sorry Ching." Ching had a soft spot after all. He told me not to ever sell my body for money. When I stopped crying, I explained to Big Boy how bad I wanted to be in the modeling contest. I only had 100 dollars, and I needed makeup, clothes, shoes and money for the hotel, and I couldn't find a job. Ching got closer. I flinched thinking he would hit me again. But he grabbed my hand and sat next to me and said, "Schoolgirl all you had to do was ask for the money, and you know I would have hooked you up." "Listen girl you are a smart, beautiful black woman and selling your body will get you only three places dead, in jail or dying of AIDS." You have parents who love you and you are doing the one thing that many of us wish we had and chance to do, you are getting a chance to be educated. "I am street smart, but being educated is one thing that no one can take away from you, you hear me girl?" I smiled and blinked my dewy wet eyelashes and said, "Yes." Ching said, "You are like the little sister that I never had." "That's why we look after you and protect you, because we known that one day you will be something special." You could be a doctor or lawyer if you just keep your head in those books." "Remember that dude Jalil that took nude pictures of you and you told us how he tricked you and to you he would give you free pictures but was just a dirty old man?" "Well, me and The Boys paid him a little visit." Not only did we beat him down and throw him in as dumpster, but we burned down that studio. "We did it all for you, our little sister." "I am not down with old perverts preying on young ladies cause it make me think of my daughter." "The thought of anyone hurting my Angel would be hell for the world." "School girl, I just don't want to see you hurt or dead, cause me and The Boys really care about you." "Now promise me you will stop all the madness and will walk the straight and narrow." I said, "I promise Ching." Ching asked me to massage his hands and feet, and stated that he would give me a special bonus." When I finished, it was late, and I said, "Well it is late and I got a lot of homework." As I headed towards the door Big Boy said "Hey schoolgirl you forgot your tip." I smiled and walked towards him expecting at least twenty five to thirty dollars. Ching reached in his pocket like he normally does and counted out one thousand dollars. My eyes were big as saucers. He said, "Take it girl before I change my mind." This is an investment into your future as the next supermodel" I believe you have the beauty and the brains to win that contest, so go make us proud." I scooped up all of the money. I thanked him and sang all the way home. I just knew I was going to finally make it as a super model, and get that shot at stardom that I longed for.

Mamma went with me to Tampa, Florida for the model search and after three days of prancing in front of the judges and being treated like a show dog today was finally judgment day. Today, all two thousand of us hopefuls found out if we were worthy of representation by the top modeling agencies. I t came down to the wire for me and I realized that no one wanted a skinny little black girl. I held my breath just praying that somebody, anybody would call my number but no one did. Finally, I started to walk off the stage with so much hurt in my eyes my number was called. I was in shock. I didn't even hear my number read. The girl next to me said, "Are you number 235204?" I said, "Yes." She said, "Girl they are calling you." "Girl you got picked!" I started screaming and jumping up and down like I had won the lottery. I was finally on my way to stardom. After returning from my modeling journey I decided to just return to my normal boring life. I was so excited to tell Phats, Big Boy and the boys the news. I went to the studio and I ran into one of the boys, his name was Rat. Rat just stared at me blankly and said, "Schoolgirl big boy told me he don't want you to come around here no more." I said, "What?" "Why?" "Did I do something wrong where's Ching?" "He will have your head for this!" I didn't matter how loud I yelled, Rat was not letting me into the studio. Finally, Rat got pissed at me and yelled, "I SAID GET THE HELL OUTTA HERE AND DON'T BRING YOUR ASS BACK EVER!" I got into my car, and I called Phats on my new cell phone. I told him what Rat told me and Phats paused and then told me that he and I couldn't hang out as friends anymore and none of his friends wanted me around anymore. I couldn't believe what Phats was telling me. As I hung up the phone, I was so confused, sad and hurt. I drove to Phat's house and Daddy Ching was there. Phats then said " Fari we don't want you to come around us no mo!" I didn't understand what was happening. All I could think is what did I do? Did I do something wrong? What was this happening? I scanned Phats and Ching with my eyes waiting for them to smile and break out in tribal laughter. Phats and Ching were known pranksters and would fool me all the time. Neither Ching nor Phats cracked a smile and I knew they were serious. I found enough air in the back of my throat to finally utter, " Well what did I do?" I was confused sad and just astonished by the words I was hearing. At this point, Phats because extremely annoyed with me and yelled " SCHOOLGIRL I SAID GO! LEAVE! NOW! LEAVE BEFORE I HAVE TO PICK YOU UP AND THROW YOU OUT!" I grabbed my backpack and walked to the door as fast as I could. Fear took over my body like a screaming banshee in a spooky forest. I fought back the tears of confusion, hate and just disappointment. Whatever I had done, I knew it landed me a one way ticket to nowhere Ville. Why were my friends turning against me? I drove home slowly that day in the warm summer rain of Florida. I rolled down the window and stuck my arm out as I cried like I lost a beloved soul. The tears began to stream down my face land the rain felt like cold tears of shame. I was mourning the loss of more than just my buddies but little did I know, I was grieving a greater loss only I didn't know. That night I cried myself to sleep. All my friends, ripped out of my heart. I didn't know why?

A week went by, and I missed the Phats and the boys. This particular day was so strange. The morning started like any other morning but something felt so strange. I was eating cereal in front of the TV just before school and the news came on. I almost choked on my cereal, when I saw who was on the TV. It was Rat and The Boys and someone had died. I saw Rat and The Boys in handcuffs being escorted by the drug enforcement officers. It felt like a ton of bricks smacked me in the face. . As I turned up the TV I sat in a deafening silence as if my ears were turned on high. , I heard the news anchor say the Daddy Ching had been found dead in a dumpster. He had been tortured with fire, beaten to death and dismembered. They found his toes, penis and his tongue ripped off and placed in a bowl on the kitchen counter of the condo he was found in. I couldn't believe what I was hearing. I was shocked to find out that Daddy Ching was a big time drug dealer, and the boys were his henchmen. I had been hanging out with drug dealers and henchmen and was so naïve that I didn't even know. The sad part is that they were good guys with good hearts who just got a bad deal in life. Most of the boys got anywhere from ten to thirty years in prison. I was sickened and saddened by the news because I finally realized that Phats, Ching and The Boys really did love me and were my friends. They protected me because they knew the end was near for them. They protected me, their little sister. All I could do is hang my head and cry and thank God that I was nowhere around when the cops took the boys out. I would've been in prison along with them not even knowing why. I lost touch with Phats and I have heard that he is now strung out on crack. I went to visit one of the boys who got away and was also a local rapper that Ching and the boys were using to launder money. His name was Tino and his rap partner Jizzim. Tino fell off the scene real quick. One day, I dropped by to see him. Tino was so jumpy and nervous like a whore in church. Tino kept peeping out of windows and acting really strange. We watched homemade sex tapes that he made of himself and they hoochie hoes he had slept with. I never saw Tino again after that day life went on for me. I saw Jizzim working in a local grocery store about three years ago. I guess his dream of being famous landed him as a bag boy. I hear Jizzm has eight children and his wife walked off and left him for another man.

TALK SHOWS ARE US

Three years later, I realized that if you were not a skinny white girl, one would probably never make it as a supermodel, at least not in Florida. My modeling jobs became fewer and fewer and I became less and less interested in being a model. I walked away from my dream of modeling and fell into a deep depression. One day, while watching my favorite talk show Montel Williams, I decided that I would write to the show just to see if they would respond. The show not only contacted me, but I ended up on the show with a girl I didn't even know. I was the mastermind and I had fabricated the whole story along with the producers egging me on. At that moment, I realized that I had a talent that, I had never realized. I had the gift of gab and I was a pretty good writer. Hell, I received all A's in my English and writing classes, but I never took any of my skills seriously. I decided to write to other talk shows just for fun. Most would respond once or twice, but I never hit the jackpot like I did with Montel. To be honest, I didn't want to be on another talk show because they make you look like a walking buffoon. Years later, my skills finally landed me in the jackpot of all jackpots. I ended up on the Oprah show. I am the biggest fan of reality TV. American idol was one of my favorite shows. I swear, I dialed my phone millions of times to help my American Idol Rueben Studdard to try to help him win. I decided that I was going to write to Oprah and tell her about my Rueben. Of course, I knew I had to spice it up, and make the letter sincere dreamy and real interesting. As I typed this letter at about three in the morning, I chuckled and laughed out lout at all of the sappy and ooey gooey lovey dovey words that I had laid it on thick in this letter. I said to myself, "Never in a million years would the Oprah show call me and have me on the show with such a stupid letter." I was sure that the show would get a good laugh at my letter. Besides, I had written to the Oprah show millions of times about every topic in the world. The most I ever received were stupid Oprah postcards and emails on occasion from her staff or a call or two. Most of the time the Oprah staff would call and ask for pictures or ask a question, but I would never hear from them again. Well about three or four months later, I was riding in my car and my cell phone rang. It was the Oprah show. I wasn't even excited because this was routine for me. I pretended I was so interested, excited, squealed, giggled and answered all of the questions with delight. I knew that there wasn't a fat chance in hell that I would ever get a chance on TV with Oprah. A few days later, as I was attending the gay days event in Orlando I received a call from the Oprah show. This time they were asking me to come to Chicago to be on the show. I was in pure shock and I started jumping up and down like a crazy jackrabbit. I was so excited to have a chance to be on the Oprah show. I have always adored Oprah and I really did love Rueben's music, but I guess I can say, I am not wife material. The strangest thing then happened. I spoke to my job and my bosses told me that they thought that they wouldn't allow me to go to the show. I was furious and devastated. I remember crying my eyes out because my only opportunity in the world to be on Oprah felt as if it was being ripped out of my hear. I was crying so hard because I thought that my bosses were the biggest jerks ever for telling me that I couldn't go to Chicago. This was a once and a lifetime thing and I was determined that I was not going to miss my opportunity. If I had to quit my job and go or pay the price of being reprimanded. I was willing to take the consequences. While I was still crying, I decided to call the Oprah show and see if they could help me persuade my bosses to let me go. This was one of the biggest mistakes I have ever made. The show called me back and asked me about the message I left. I couldn't believe what I was hearing. Oprah's producers thought that I was mentally ill and that I could be a security issue. I thought to myself are they kidding me? I explained to her producer that, I was terribly upset because of my bosses saying no. I thought maybe they could talk to my bosses, so I could attend the show. For petes sake, I mean this was the Oprah show and not Hank's underground garage show. I guess the show finally realized that I wasn't a nutcase just a regular girl who was about to embark on a journey that few have taken and lived to tell about. Finally, the Oprah Show approved for me to come and I was ecstatic. I was on my way to the Oprah Show. My writing to her show for at least ten years had finally paid off. I had about twenty-four hours to get ready for the show. I decided that I would take out my braids and wear my natural hair. I went to a local drag queen that is also a hairdresser. Starlina is a well-known drag queen in Florida who just so happens to be a hairdresser. I decided I wanted to get the Oprah Winfrey haircut. Everybody knows Oprah has the best hair. I too wanted my hair to have a million layers with the Oprah shine and bounce. Starlina relaxed my hair to perfection and then turned me away from the mirror. I can still hear the horrifying sound of the scissors. All I could hear is a horrifying snip, snip, snip, SNIP! When Starlina was finished she spun around the chair and I damn near fainted at what I saw. My shoulder length tresses were now up to my ears. I could've just died! I asked for an Oprah Winfrey cut with tons of layers just like Oprah. Can you believe this fool gave me an Opie Wood tree cut! It was the worst hairdo ever and lucky me I had to wear it on national television. For the world to see my rats nest hair of disaster. I was so upset about my hair, but I still had to buy a dress, and heels and make my flight to Chicago. I ran in a well-known upscale department store and I yelled to the sales person "I was going on the Oprah Show." I hoped mentioning Oprah's name would that would get me quick service. I must say saying the name Oprah gets you impeccable service. I bought this beautiful ice blue dress with sparkling heels. I the airport I rushed and I thought I would miss my flight. My flight was delayed for an hour. I chatted with a nearby curious family who asked me where I was going. I proudly said " I'm gonna be on the Oprah show". Why I said that well I found out the hard way of what happens when you mention Oprah's name around the common folk. People started surrounding me like hornets doing the mating dance. There was one woman who passed me a note and began to tell the sob story of her sick grandson and honestly I tuned her out. I had just been Oprah-sized! Meaning, I now know what Oprah goes through on a daily basis with all the beggin and bugging that the do to get help from Oprah. People were begging, pleading and giving me messages to give Oprah. I even went to the bathroom to escape people and all of their questions because it just became too much. A woman actually stuck a note under my bathroom stall door that said, "Dear Oprah on it." I felt so bad that I couldn't really help these people. After about thirty minutes on the plane, I still had people coming over to bother me about the show. I was so annoyed, but I understood that I was fortunate enough to experience didn't happen to many people. I stayed humble and kind throughout the entire experience. On the plane I was really frustrated the curious family kept approaching me, and people continued to come and sit next to me or yell across their seats to ask me questions or ask favors. I was so overwhelmed by all of the attention and aggravation of it all. Finally, I pretended to go to sleep and I kept my eyes closed the entire flight. One or two times, I was awakened by other passengers and asked questions. I was at peace and finally. I could hear the deafening silence of the plane roaring its way to Chicago. I drifted off to sleep and when I awoke, I was in Chicago. I decided after my plane experience, I was going to keep the whole Oprah thing quiet. I learned the hard way that Oprah has an extremely powerful name and it was nothing to toy with. I guess a commoner like myself didn't know that. I certainly know better now. I am convinced that people go crazy or go into some type of mad trance when Oprah's name is mentioned. I finally just pretended like I was asleep so that people would just leave me alone. I was eerily calm when I arrived in Chicago and man was it cold. It was July and it was freezing. I didn't have coat and I had on short shorts. I decided to put heavy clothing in my mental notes the next time I visited Chicago. A woman with a two-way radio met me at the doors of the airport and she escorted me to a beautiful black stretch limo that Oprah sent me. It was beautiful. I was so happy yet sad. No one else was there with me to share the experience. I rolled down the windows and I waived and yelled at any strangers that would pass by. When I got to my hotel it was not the one I thought it would be but you could tell it was and expensive and old like the titanic. I nicknamed that place the titanic because to me the place was old and spooky. It had the smell of old world war two ghosts. This hotel had leather couches and chairs with huge buttons and huge burgundy oak tables. It kind of reminded you of your old great grandfather's study. I wasn't thrilled about this hotel but it was my new home for the night. The elevator was extremely small and the hallways were smaller and so quiet that, I felt like I was at church. I went to my room and I was pretty happy with my beautiful room. It was quaint with two huge beds. I felt much better and not as afraid one I saw the room. Once I got settled into the hotel, I realized that I was pretty hungry. I called downstairs for room service and was told they were closed. I couldn't believe that my one freebie meal was snatched away by time. So I devised a plan. There were complimentary robes in the closet. I decided to walk to the nearest store to buy a jacket in my complimentary bathrobe of course! As I was walking a bellhop yelled out "Hey beautiful." Where are you going in that bathrobe?" I was hoping that no one would notice me but my luck had just run out. The three bellhops motioned for me to come over and cha. I put on my nasty don't bother me attitude but I still went over to embark on this adventure. I quickly explained that I was in town for the Oprah Show. All of the bellhops laughed at me and thought I was lying. I walked away, cold annoyed and just ready to get where I was going. Who cares if those idiots didn't believe me? At that moment, I realized I was Oprahsized again and that I really had to stop using her name for anything because it got me in world of trouble. As I briskly walked away from the bellhops one of them yelled out "Hey can I take you out on a date tonight?" I told him maybe and walked off. He ran behind me and said, "No I am serious." I will pick you up in my car. I told him no because he was a stranger and I was not getting into a car with him. I finally agreed to go out with this guy but only if we walked to the restaurant. My philosophy of this whole date thing was Heck, I was broke in Chicago alone and the hotel kitchen was closed. Lets just say free food is always a plus! The restaurant that we went to had horrible food was dirty and the service was worse. While playing with my horrific food I thought "This guy didn't have a chance in hell with me." I knew I it was a fraud and this unsuspecting fella had no clue that all I wanted was free dinner. Sometimes looking like a femme woman has its perks, so I just used what I've got to get what I wanted. Heck guys do that to women to get what they want all the time. I kept my secret lesbian life to myself and pretended to show interest this strange man. After dinner we walked back to my hotel and this guy turned out to really be nice and after dinner I took a picture of him and never saw this man again. We spoke on the phone twice. After that I lost his number and truly had no interest in him. The night before the Oprah Show, I couldn't sleep a wink. I remember being scared. I was alone in the spookiesville horror hotel. I was kind of nervous and afraid. I thought I would oversleep and miss the taping of the show. I tossed and turned all night long till finally the alarm went off and they day of glory finally arrived. After two hours of sleep and a prayer, I got dressed for the Oprah Show. I made the best of the hair from hell and I put on my prom dress look alike. I dressed alone in my room for the Oprah Show and couldn't get my zipper up. I knocked on the next door in my hotel for assistance. The person in the room looked at me funny but I explained to them that I was alone and in town to do the Oprah Show. This woman assisted me with a smile and I thanked her. I was so excited, but I didn't have any fear. The staff in the hotel was so nice and I told them that I was waiting on my limo from the Oprah Show. They were all so sweet. One girl even painted my nails at the front desk for me while I waited. There was a woman, who reminded me of Fran Dresher approached me in the lobby. As I was waiting, she asked me to take a picture with her. I really felt like a celebrity that day and I loved every minute of it. Finally, after about 20 minutes of waiting my black shiny stretch limo arrived. I hopped in and off we went to Harpo Studios. I was so excited and didn't have a care in the world. As I rode alone to Harpo Studios, I snapped photos of myself because I was so afraid that no one would ever believe that I was way on the Oprah Show. I guess I didn't think about the fact that millions of people watch her show. As I arrived with the other guests we went thought security and they took my camera and my modeling photo that I autographed to give to Oprah. Needless to say her staff confiscated all of my gifts for her and my camera. As we proceeded to the waiting room, I met some of the sweetest people. I met a woman and her daughter. They explained to me that they were the ones that were responsible for Clay Aiken auditioning for American Idol. They were so excited and I even took a picture with them standing near the limo. They told me that they had never been in a limo in their lives and this was a once in a lifetime chance for them. I also met several little girls in red shirts who were so cute and giggly. I would say they were maybe thirteen years old or so. They helped me make my sign for Rueben that said, "Forget the girls in red marry me instead." What a joke! How could I continue with this lesbian in a straight woman's dress fraud? Who was I kidding? I thought to myself, "Hmm who would ever believe that I was straight and in love with a man even if he was famous?"

The Oprah staff came in to brief us on what to do and then we were off to the makeup room. Everyone was being primped and powdered when one of Oprah's staff members asked me what I was wearing. I was baffled by her question. Was this lady blind? Did she not see the beautiful dress I was wearing? At first, I thought this lady was kidding but unfortunately she wasn't. I told her that I was already dressed and that was that. I paid bazillion dollars for my outfit and this lady had the audacity to ask me, "What I was wearing for the show?" My mama and all my friends were watching. I had to be presentable. As we were ushered into Oprah's studio, I remember being excited yet not impressed. The studio was quite small but I was happy to be there. I was seated on the front row. All of a sudden there was the countdown five, four, three two one and were live in Chicago and on national TV. I remember the studio roaring with cheers and claps when Oprah came out and everything was a quiet hush. Oprah was talking, but I sewer I could hardly hear a word Oprah was saying. I was looking at Oprah and wondering is she was a robot. She barely blinked or moved her head. Before, we were brought to by Oprah's staff, we were told to only speak to her if she spoke to us. I patiently waited for Oprah to call on me. I had a secret that even Oprah didn't know. I knew I had made up my straight persona even though I was in fact a fan of Rueben and I loved American Idol. I had a secret. I knew in my heart that the swooning letter that I had sent to the show was a partial fraud. I was pretending that I was interested in this man and that I thought of him as a future husband or boyfriend. As the world watched Oprah read my letter on national television about Rueben. The syrupy dreamboat fraud graced the television of millions. I sat there in shock and in shame. I knew my sisters back in Florida were proud of me, but they all knew I was a fraud. I was a big old lesbian fraud. I had pulled off the biggest TV film flam ever! I was faking who and what I was because I knew I was a lesbian pretending. I was not the swooning straight woman that I portrayed. I was a big ole lesbian and I knew it! I remember making a sign that says forget the girls in red marry me instead. Who exactly was I kidding? I remember Oprah was reading something, but I could barely hear her. Halfway through the letter I realized it was the letter I had written to the show about Rueben. Oprah kept calling me the wrong name. I think I was in shock and I did nothing more than smile and blink. I made a total fool out of myself on national television. Oprah's staff then did something that upset Rueben and myself. The staff moved me away from Rueben by changing my seat location. I was placed behind a camera where no one could see me and a Caucasian woman was place next to Rueben. Rueben Studdard protested but I didn't say a word. I remember Rueben asked if I could take his seat and he even got up like a gentleman to give me his seat. Rueben was so kind and such a southern gentleman. Oprah's staff ignored Rueben's pleads for me to sit next to him and then they counted down back from commercial. I took my seat. My face was so heated with anger. I couldn't believe that I had been dissed on the Oprah Show, and Rueben Studdard from American Idol witnessed the whole thing. I am positive that Oprah to this day does not know her staff mistreated me the way they did and that a fellow celebrity witnessed it and nothing was done to stop it. During the show, I sat there smiling but I was pretty pissed at this point and ready to just hop a plane and leave. I never had a chance to talk to Rueben or even have a moment alone to talk to him. I felt bamboozled because the producers of the show made it seem as if I would get a chance to at least have a conversation with Rueben. I really was a fan of Rueben just not in love. Yet, I did find him kinda cute. At that moment when I locked eyes with Rueben I thought to myself maybe just maybe I could fall for a nice guy like Rueben. I found that I was attracted to this man even though I was a practicing lesbian. There were two women who were sitting right behind me and they witnessed the entire horrible incident. They were pretty upset too because it really was not fair, that I came to meet Rueben, but someone else ended up sitting with him. Even Rueben said out loud that it wasn't fair that I had come so far to see him. They treated me away like a red headed stepchild. Maybe Oprah thought, I sucked as a guest. I was extremely tired after my long night staying at the creepy hotel the show put me up in. I remembered the smell of old leather and wood. Just the thought of that hotel gave me chills. As I snapped back from my hotel of horror daydream the Oprah Show taping was over. The two women sitting behind me approached me and expressed their displeasure of how the Oprah staff treated me. They asked me if I would like to have lunch with them and Rueben at the local radio station. These women were the program director and her assistant of a local Chicago radio station. Without even thinking I jumped at the chance to finally hang out with Rueben since the show had let me down and left me high and dry. I was truly bamboozled. I guess, I deserved it for what I had done. It's not nice to fool Oprah, but I couldn't tell the world that I was a lesbian. I mean, heck my mama and all her church members were watching. I surely didn't want to embarrass or shame my family. I called the Oprah show and told them that I was ditching her limo. I put on my pink and white girlie tracksuit with matching shoes. The radio station sent me a car and off I was to meet Rueben, so I thought. When I got to the radio station there was so much chaos in the lobby. I lost my souvenir sign that I had on the show. I finally somehow made it into the studio and was escorted to a room. To my surprise there was a room full of about 100 of Ruben's favorite listeners, media and staff of the radio station. They were ordering people all around and I got shoved all around the room and never got a chance to say one word to Rueben. We locked eyes with each other and he acknowledged each other. His brother waived to me. Rueben was then rushed out of the room and a mob of people surrounded him. I felt so empty and so sad because once again I lost my chance to meet and talk to Rueben. For two hours, I asked the receptionist to page the two women that asked me to come to the station. Neither woman ever showed their faces. I was pretty upset that I had traveled so far to meet Rueben and this was turning into a disaster. I officially was stranded in Chicago and didn't have dime to get home. The Oprah Show told me that if I missed my plane I was responsible for getting myself home. I realized at this point that I had made a very stupid decision. The two women that invited me to the radio station just simply vanished and I begged the staff of the radio station to help me find these two ladies. The receptionist kept paging them. Finally, one sent up a message telling me to ride the subway. What in the world would I know about a subway? I was from Florida and I didn't know the first thing about a subway. I was also flat broke so that was not an option. Finally, after about two and a half hours of being abandoned an on air personality from the station felt sorry for me and drove me to the airport. He gave me all kinds of tee shirts and hats and stuff to make up to me what happened. We rode in the company vehicle and to the airport. People kept honking at us because we were in a radio station vehicle and I guess they thought we had prizes or something. I just smiled giggled and waived. On our way to the airport we talked about ourselves. We then got on "the conversation." I knew the lesbian talk was coming and I admitted that I was a lesbian and he told me it was cool. I made it to the airport thanks to this angel from the radio station in the sky. I always wonder what happened to this guy and would love to see him just to thank him for saving a foolish girl from another state. I was so relieved to step on the plan and head home. The flight back to Florida was the worst. There was a horrible thunder and lightning storm and the plane dipped, dropped, bobbed and weaved in the dark clouds and pouring rain. It felt like we were on a plane headed straight for hell. I was certain I was going to die that day and my claim to fame would be the girl in the prom dress who went on the Oprah Show, got dissed and then died in a plane crash. I guess that would've made national news. There was a baby on the plane with blood curding screams and he whimpers. The baby screamed at the top of his lungs during the whole flight. I felt like I wanted to scream and cry too. But of course I couldn't. Finally, I made it back to Florida in one piece. I could've French kissed the ground; boy was I grateful to see my beloved Florida. Life after Oprah was not pleasant and I didn't get hooked up with a billionaire like the stupid crowing rooster lady that was in the audience a few years ago. Lucky me. I got the grand prize, and boy was it a whammy! The next day while listening to Rueben's cd and singing and reminiscing, I was pulled over by the police and I got a two hundred and fifty dollar speeding ticket. A week later, I lost my job. Then my car broke down. While on unemployment, I had to file bankruptcy. I couldn't afford to pay all my bills. I had harassing calls from creditors and then attorneys started calling and threatening. I finally broke down and filed bankruptcy. In my heart, I couldn't help but be envious of all of those people who have went on the Oprah Show and walked away with billion dollar husband and chances to interview celebrities and great gifts and prizes. I decided why dwell on it? My life has been a horror story. If I didn't have bad luck I wouldn't have any luck at all. So why would I expect anything other than drama, problems and a miserable life? I still love the Oprah Show and watch it everyday despite the awful things that happened to me during my visit to her show. I can say that her staff hurt my feelings. I was highly disappointed, but I will always love Oprah. I have always looked at Oprah as a mother figure and have written to her since I was about ten years old. I have always had a fantastic mother in my life. I would write to the Oprah Show weekly to tell them things that I wouldn't ever tell my mother. I will always feel like I have connection with Oprah, because she is so kind, giving and just a gracious soul. One day I would love to chat with her again and share my experience. My biggest regret was that I never had a chance to tell Oprah how sorry I was for pretending to be straight and lying to the world about my sexuality. I also feel horrible that I ditched her limo that she so graciously sent to me. I look at Oprah as a mentor, a mother, and a teacher. I appreciate all the great things she has done for so many. From Oprah I have learned to be a humanitarian and just love the world. Thank you so much Oprah for just being you. By the way Oprah, I am really sorry for what I did and I hope one day to face you, so that I can apologize and write you out a check for the damage I caused or at least work off my debt to you. Until we meet again Oprah.

OPRAH WINFREY

By, Rose Sutra

Oprah is all that and then some...

This magnetic talk show host has hypnotized the world to the sound

Of her media drum

By captivating and educating peoples minds out of the humdrum

And bring light to those humans that had none

It's Oprah with the highest scale in pay!

Multi millionaire that's what the magazines say

She makes Donald Trump want to sing the blues

Ms. Winfrey has paid her dues

But there were times when she had it tough

And it was her father, who disciplined her out of the ruff

She was able to release her childhood pain of sexual abuses and rape

She fought hard to over come the hate

For now she views the world with a happier mental state.

Oprah is all that an then some

She graduated from Tennessee State University and later went on to

become Radio Announcer, reporter and news anchor

For her career did not stop there

This marked the turning point where destiny became clear

The Oprah Winfrey Show was born and syndicated throughout the world

Oprah you go girl, Oprah you go girl!

Starring in the movie Color Purple in 1985, her actress career kicked live

In 1989, she later showed her face in the hit T.V. serious The Women of Brewster Place

Maintaining her success with faness, in 1984 she was blessed to inducted into the hall of fame because Oprah played the game!

CHAPTER III

ON MY BEDROOM WALL

By Rose Sutra

She was a unique super doper sex freak between the sheets,

She made my womb energy leak all over her diamond mountain peek.

My orgasm underground tunnel deep, she hit my gee, she made me tweak,

like a well-written poetry piece!

How could I resist when she was nine inches steep, deep, I bet she got

mad girlz on the creep for a piece?

She look like a Black Madonna Jesus, for many reasons she kept me hot

like a New York summer season!

Splash, she took a dive and went down on my pyramid mound, look who

bless the queen now!

I gave her applause as she took her bows, "wow" milk the cow!

She had me aroused like ecstasy, her tongue felt like a strong bottle of

Hennessey, mixed with coke, she rocked my boat, kept my clit on float,

long tongue, no hat, most real women like it like that!

I got cha # on my bedroom wall, I'm a call you when I need another hit quick!

MY ONE-NIGHT STANDS

By, Rose Sutra

I called these escapades my one-night stands because they weren't real relationships. A real relationship to me is over one year together. Getting to know and grow with that one special person.

JENNIE

I met her at a lesbian nightclub, located in Queens New York called "Hatfeilds." I was dressed in a tight Minnie skirt, pumps, short haircut, lace blouse, face made up and hair done. I was going to catch a cutie tonight. I saw her in the club. She was just my type for the night, a Spanish butch. Jennie was about five foot six; very light skinned, brown eyes, straight light-brown hair, a cancer, and about 165 pounds. I cruised her. I guess she liked what she saw, because she asked me to dance. We talked and exchanged phone numbers after our dance. Jennie called me. We went out with my Gay mother Sandra and Deedee. We all met up at my house in Queens New York. From there we had went to a restaurant in Nassau County Long Island. We ate, talked and laughed throughout dinner. After dinner, Deedee left and went home, but Jennie and I went back to Sandra's house to have sex. She was good in bed as I thought. Jennie licked my twat well, but when I tried to go down on her, Jennie told me no. I guess that is a butch thing? So I let her fuck the shit out of me. All I remember was that it felt like a fantasy. We had sex until daybreak in my gay momma's apartment on her son's twin bed. Now that was ghetto, and we both were hoer's, but that's what you do when you are young and hot. We never had a relationship. We were two passing ships in the night. I had seen her around in clubs with other woman. Oh well, on to my next conquest!

TOYA

Toya was a Scorpio, about five feet; short curly hair, honey complexion, a Correction Officer and hard butch. I meet her through my friend Edward, who has died from HIV Aids. We all three were sitting around talking and drinking. Edward said, "I think you two would be good together." I did not know this woman, but I ended up that night kissing her in Edwards's room. I would not label her relationship material, but the sex was darn good. I had never in my life been bent over a stair banister and fucked up my ass like fagot. She banged me so intensely that when I bent over forward, all I saw was cum running out of my twat down to the floor. That was so fierce! This chick could really fuck. And she knew it. Toya was a butch hoe. She constantly kept me coming back for more. But, then again she was always high off something. I knew she was seeing other women, but who cared. Personally, I just needed to get fucked! And that was all it ever was, a fuck. Until, she one day said, "I am going to get an apartment, and I want you to move in with me." I told her no. The last I heard, she moved to California. Toya gave me the best ass fuck; I ever had in my entire life.

VANESSA

Vanessa lived in Far Rock Queens, New York. She was five foot seven, Spanish, short straight hair cut, light skinned, very fem, nice thin body, and a hoer. I met her through my gay mother Sandra. We all hung out at the same club ever Friday night the Cubby Hole or Crazy Nanny's. Sandra had already slept with her and really liked her. I didn't know that Vanessa liked me too, until the night of my earth birthday. Vanessa had given me blue leather Minnie dress as a present for my birthday. I told her thank you. Since this was my birthday weekend, I celebrated with all my lesbian friends at Tracks, a gay nightclub in Manhattan in New York We partied, and drank, until four in the morning. Since Vanessa rode with me to the club that night, I also had to drop her back home. When Vanessa had got into my car, she had also brought another hard dyke with her. I said to myself, "What the fuck is going on here?" They both got in. I started the car and pulled off. Ten minutes later I look in rear view mirror, and Vanessa and this girl is making out. I was already drunk, but now I am tripping. I said to myself, "No this bitch did not, right in the back seat of my car!" I did not say anything to her. After they had finishing kissing, Vanessa said, "Can you drop her off first?" So I did. Once we dropped Vanessa's friend off, Vanessa got in the front seat. She told that she wanted me to come in. So I did. When I got in, she asked me to have sex with her. So I did. During sex, she asked me to ball my fist up and shove it up her pussy! Now at this point, I said, "Whatever, this bitch is a hoer, and I can get the experience. For the record, I will never ever, ever, ever stick my fist up another woman's vagina! I felt body parts I never felt before. It grossed me out. When I pulled out my hand it was covered with all this white stuff. I ran to the bathroom, turned the water on and that was nasty. Vanessa said, "Oh no you are just a baby." She meant that I had no experience, and she was right. That was the last time I ever saw Vanessa. I will always remember my fist coming out of her twat.

ANGIE

Dam, this straight woman was fine. I knew the first day I had met her that I would lick her pussy. Angie was five foot seven, sandy brown short dread locks, big but, nice body, funny, brown eyes, and married. I met her by performing at her business. Angie and husband called me up to start a poetry venue at their establishment. They agreed to pay me ever Saturday night for four hours of entertainment. I put on a poetry successful show for about two months. While I was doing this, I was also getting to know

Angie. I did not know that this would be the last show. She told me that night about twelve midnight that they were selling their business. I was kind of sad. So Angie and I talked for about two hours in the shop. We drove her son home first. Then she drove me home. We sat in her jeep and talked for about another half hour. She had asked me what is it like to get your pussy eaten? I said, "Do you want me to show you?" She said, "Yes." I leaned over and started to kiss her tenderly on her lips. She began to kiss me back. I started touching her all over her body. My fantasy finally came true. I was banging Angie in the front seat of her jeep. She was so hot. She unbuttoned her jeans. I pulled them down. I continued to open and smell her vagina. I smelled good. I started licking, sucking, and eating her pussy non-stop until she screamed and had an orgasm. She came in five minutes. Here I go again drunk and feeling these women. She finally told me to stop. She jumped up and said, "I got to go home before my husband comes looking for me." I got out of her jeep and went upstairs to my apartment. Two hours later I started throwing up. I felt like I was on death's bed. I called my friend Meme and told her that I finally fucked Angie. Meme said, "You don't sound to great." I replied, "I feel like I am going to die." Meme said, "You ate some nasty ass pussy." I replied, "Angie's pussy did not smell nasty." However, Angie and I spoke over the phone twice after that experience. She told me that she needed a place to stay. She was breaking up with her husband. I really could not help her at the time. I told Angie that I really don't have any space for another person in my apartment. After that phone conversation, I never saw her again.

RACHELL

I met Rachel while I attended York College in Queens New York playing basketball. I thought she was so cute. She was Spanish, light skinned, long sandy blonde curly hair, five foot six, 160 pounds, green eyes and some big tata's (breast). We started hanging out together, riding bikes, going to the movies, having lunch and talking over the phone. She really liked me to the point where she was stalking me. At the time I did not care, because I liked her too. We kissed a lot. I refused to have sex with her. One, she was a married a man. Two, I did not like her body. Three, at the time I was really feeling someone else. Well, my roommate had gone out of town for a week. I had invited Rachel over for a while. I cooked lunch and we talked. I was really feeling hot so we sat on the couch and started kissing. I was going to have sex with her, but once she took off here blouse I did not like her body. At the point, I just sucked her big ass breasts and put hickey's all over her neck. She asked me, "why didn't I go down on her?" I told her that I did not feel like it. She put her dress back on and left. She called me when she had got home and told me her husband wanted to know who did she get those hickey's on neck from? Rachel told him that I did it and gave him my phone number. He called me the next morning, yelling, screaming and threatened to kill me over touching his wife. Actually, I put a great big hickey on her neck! I told him, Rachel let me touch her. He told me that he was going to get his gun, come over to my apartment and kill me! I laughed at him, and told him that I would call the cops on him. I told him to stop his wife from stalking me. "That's why I put hickey's on her neck." Rachel asked for it, I did not push myself on her. She constantly wanted me to kiss her everywhere we went. Up on the roof at York College, in the movies she wanted to finger me, on the beach and practically everywhere we went she wanted to get busy. That's what I told her husband. He hung up the phone and left me alone. Rachel and I never hung out again. We only spoke in passing.

BRENDA

I met Brenda in the Village in New York City. We both were very much attracted to one another. She was totally fem. She was dark skinned, long black hair, nice body, beautiful personality, and brown eyes. As usually every Saturday I went to West 4th Street in Manhattan New York. During the 1990's, that was the meeting ground for most lesbian women.

I went down to catch the girls play basketball. There she was, miss honey in some hot shorts. I walked over to her and complimented her outfit. I then introduced myself. She told me her name, and we started chatting. I asked Brenda if she wanted to go to the beach. She said, "Sure." So we walked back to my car and head for Jones Beach. While we were driving, we talked a lot about each other. We were both hot in the pants, so I pulled the car over to side of the highway, and we got busy. We stared kissing, hugging, and Brenda started taking off her cloths. Boy was she hot! I started licking her breast, touching her stomach, kissing on her neck, and caressing her vagina. We were so totally into each other that we had forgot where we were. Brenda had taken off all her cloths, and told me to eat her pussy. So I did. While all this sex action was taking place, the Nassau County State Troopers were watching us. The Trooper knocked on the steamy window. He said, "Excuse me ladies is everything all right?" At this point, I look up and said "Oh shit" shocked as heck. I said, "Brenda put on your dress right now." Brenda looked at me, saying, "Where is my dress; I don't have any panties on; do not open that window; cover me up." This was one of the most embarrassing moments every. The state trooper just stood there waiting for us to roll down the window. I told the state trooper to hold on for one minute. Brenda found her dress and put it on while the state trooper watched her. I rolled down the window to talk to the trooper. He said, "You know that this is illegal to pull over here young lady." I replied, "Oh I did not know that Sir." The trooper said, "I will let you go this time, but next time you will get a ticket." We rolled up the windows and continue to drive to the beach to get our groove on, ya know! That was so embarrassing. After that day I never saw Brenda again. But, she was good fuck!

MY ONE-NIGHT STANDS

By, Safari

SHORTY

My next encounter was with a WNBA player. Everyone called her Shorty.
Her real name was Breanon. Shorty was suave with the ladies. She was so
sexy and chocolate. I met shorty in a lesbian bar one night. I was with this
white girl that liked me her name was Annie. I was not feeling any white
chicks. Shorty's WNBA pal Teresa Sands told me that Shorty wanted to
meet me. I was so shocked. I ditched Annie. Shorty and I went out on
several dates and I really thought she was a nice person and was digging
me. She fooled me. I found out that she had told many lies to me and to
her friends. Shorty never told me that she had a girlfriend, whom she flew
in from Spain. She told her friends and girlfriend that I was a crazy stalker.
I couldn't believe the drama that came from this one little player with the
hell of a jump shot. The girls in my town started to hate me. They wanted
to beat me up because of my association with Shorty. She had totally
dissed me. If I ever saw Shorty again, I would give her the ole one, two-
punch right in the kisser just for the trouble she caused me.

NYREEN

I met another WNBA player at a lesbian party. I was really confused by
her because when I met her I was not sure if she was gay. After going out

with her a few times and spending a lot of long nights with Octavia, I still was not sure about her sexuality. One night while sitting in a car during late night chitchat, she reached over and started rubbing my leg. I told her that I felt she was flirting with me. She made me feel like the biggest fool. She acted so surprised and apologized for making me think she was anything other than straight.

A few months later, I found out the truth, as we were in bed having wild hot sex and she was working the hell out of a strap on dildo. I remember her sweating on top of me as I said, "You may think you are fooling the rest of the world with your straight woman claim, but I know better." She smiled and never acknowledged my words, but I knew. We continued to see each other off. I realized that I was basically her midnight booty call and breakfast partner. Several times she would leave me in hotels alone and never came back. I felt like such a dime store whore. I felt like I had no purpose.

One day while at school, one of her other women started stalking me by phone. She called day and night and harassed me. I told Octavia to get her shit straight with her hoes. I knew that I was not the only woman. I played the game accordingly. Octavia and I are still friends, but I gave up the role of midnight booty call. I started to long for a real relationship. I wanted some one on one action.

SAVON

The next woman that I dated was named Savon. She seemed to have her act together. I found out months after we were involved that not only was she crazy as hell, but she was a drug addict Savon had bricks and bricks of marijuana in her cabinets and smoked day and night. I found out Savon had cheated on me with her drug supplier, who was now a reverend. I was so mentally drained after this relationship. I fell into the arms of another woman.

KARMA

I sat back in the Florida sun and I began to think about my past and everything that made me what I was today. I was a full-fledged lesbian. I was broken and full of despair. All of my relationships with men had been so miserable. All they ever wanted was sex and more sex. I never enjoyed sex with men. It felt like an on going job or a rape that would never end. I never felt a personal or close connection with men. I knew by the time I was three years old that I didn't ever want to marry a man or be his wife. I refused to be a servant and a slave to a man for the rest of my life like my mamma. Living in Florida had liberated me. I decided that I wanted to dabble further into the world of lesbianism. I was looking for the love, respect and the social connection that I lacked with men. I felt with women I would have a special bond and a deep genuine love. My first adult experience with a woman was terrible and I remember she drugged me. This Afro wearing "Power to the people woman," named Karma was my first. I should've known with a name like Karma that trouble was yet to follow. Karma said, "She was 35 years old." I found out weeks later that she was in fact fifty-five years old. Karma and I were supposed to just be friends, so I thought. We met up with her at a party. After the party, I went to her house, so we could go to the club. The next thing I knew, I was naked with my legs spread wide open and Karma was licking and sucking on my tender hot spot. I had been drugged for sure and disoriented. I was so sick when I sat up in the bed. She had to help me to the bathroom. I threw up all the way home. I wanted nothing more to do with Karma. At the time, I had a sex fiend boyfriend and a husband, but that's another story.

Karma began stalking me and continued to stalk me for two years. One time, I went to work and my co-workers told me to take a look at my car. Do you know this crazy bitch decorated my car with lipstick and a life-sized poster of herself? She left a key inside this huge two-foot card that said, "This is a key to my house." I was scared as hell of this woman. I knew she was a crazy ticking time bomb. Crazy Karma stared leaving boxes in front of my house that would say things like, "This is a bomb and it will exploded in sixty seconds." She began to leave gifts in front of my house like it was a shrine. One day, Crazy Karma left a cake that was heart shaped. She stuck a huge butcher knife in the middle of the cake. There was a note that said, "If, I can't have you no one else will!" I had to move to try to shake this demon woman, but she found me again. I ended up having to take legal action. I had an old cop friend of mine pay her a visit. My brother wanted to go to her house and beat her down, but I knew that fool would probably kill her and hide her body or something.

I ended up kicking my sex fiend boyfriend to the curb and divorced my husband. Karma finally stopped worrying my life after the restraining order and few threats from my brother and his boys. The last I heard of Karma, was that she is now straight, has a boyfriend and is a pastor at a church. One would think, that my luck with women would have improved. The sad part is that it didn't. It only got crazier!

MARTINA

I went out on a first date with this Spanish girl named Martina. Martina was the most boring date I have ever had in my life. She was a cute little butchy girl with medium length dark hair. I really felt like Martina was hot but her boring personality was not. Martina and I went on a date to a spoken word poetry event that at a local spot. I remember that the event was pretty lame and I couldn't see a thing. We had very little conversation. The night was a total bore and I needed a drink or something to make the night better. I saw two of my friends, who knew a local poet from New York. And they wanted me to hook her up with some venues of poetry.

MR. SKYSCRAPER

I befriended a married man named Morris "Skyscraper" Wilson and he and I became some cool friends. He was and x-NBA player and I regarded him as a friend. We used to hang out at strip clubs and get pretty drunk with him and all of his friends. I could put away drinks with the rest of the fellows and they treated me like a buddy in a skirt. They used to say that's no woman that is Safari. I loved hanging out with the fellow's cause it took me away from the dreadful world of heartbreak and lesbianism. Sky was and is a married man yet a straight up cheater. He never knew that I knew his wife, his neighbors and even his children. You know the bad thing about men like Sky? He is married with children and didn't care if people knew that he had another woman. Women called Sky day and night. I remember one night hanging out with his lesbian millionaire neighbor, my girlfriend and all of their friends we were watching this movie about a threesome. After the movie Skyscraper's wife was half drunk and she kept saying over and over again how she knew her husband loved her. I just sat there and said nothing. I knew that her man was a low down dog and she was sadly mistaken. I felt sorry for this little four foot tall live in maid and kept wife. Rochelle was a kept wife. She seemed miserable. In her heart, she knew her man was a cheater but she stayed for the money, the big house and the glory. Rochelle even showed us her wedding pictures. I saw all kinds of celebrities at her wedding including Dr. J himself! As I looked at the photos, I thought how pathetic. Sky is seven feet plus inches and he married a four-foot child bride look alike that I prefer to call Frawline. Sky and I continued to hang out more and more. One night we went to the strip club and got really drunk. The next thing I know we were performing oral sex on each other. I remember thinking "What are you doing Fari?" You are a lesbian." I felt like I was caught between two worlds that I was fighting. A few weeks later, we did the oral sex thing again and after that night, I knew that I would never be with a man again. I realized that I only fooled around with Sky out of anger and hatred for him and his wife. I hated the fact that Sky betrayed the trust and the sanity of marriage. He had the privilege of marriage, and a lesbian woman like myself had no rights to marry. I also hated Rochelle his wife, because she started a huge fight with my girlfriend and I. I was messing around with her husband gave me a sense of power. It allowed me to feel the vengeance that I needed to fulfill. From this situation, I learned a lot. I learned that I am truly a lesbian. I learned that mostly all men live their lives on the low and cheat on their wives. I also learned that many married women are just stuck on stupid and keep their minds on the money. Many women out here will sell their souls to the devil to get a rich man and keep him, but most don't think that he may one day bring home AIDS and disease. I thank God everyday that I didn't pick up AIDS from this man or any of my past encounters and after this crazy incident I was positive that I wanted to be in monogamous relationship.

DARYEN

Daryen was a girl that I met on the phone chat line. I was bored in life and wanted to meet a woman to have some fun with. So the first time I met Daryen I went to her house and I made one of the biggest mistakes in my life. I didn't want to have sex, but Daryen convinced me to. I recall feeling that having sex with her was the worst ideal ever. The sex wasn't even good. About a week later, I started to feel funny and my vagina started having some strange issues and a strange odor. I told Daryen, "I think that maybe you gave me a disease." Daryen paid for me to go to her gynecologist and he told me it was a yeast infection. A week later, the symptoms came back again. I knew in my heart something was wrong. I went to my own doctor. I had the shock of my life! I found out that I had an STD! I had been careful all my life. I was always careful about who I slept with and always took care of myself. How could this happen to me? I just didn't understand. Why would Daryen do this to me? Thank goodness that is was not HIV! I went to Daryen's house to tell her my devastating news. She refused to take the chain off her door. I knew she knew something was wrong. I brought her medication. She refused to open the door. I was so pissed off that she would give me a disease and then she would just act as if she didn't even know me. Daryen was dead wrong. I got so mad that I began kicking the door. I swear, I wanted to kick it off the hinges. Five days later, I was cured. As far as I know, Daryen is still walking around passing out diseases to people. I would never in life deal with someone from the chat line again. I got more than what I bargained for and if I had a chance to do it all over again I wouldn't! I also should have taken the advise of my mother. She always told me that if a person lives in a dirty house, they probably have a dirty coochi. I will always remember dirty house dirty coochi, dirty house dirty coochi! My motto is, "If your house is dirty or the coochi don't smell right, it is time for me to live disease free." After dealing with this nasty woman, I became very cautious and very afraid of women, men and sex. I didn't want to be the next AIDS patient nor the next victim. I didn't have sex for a long, long time after this awful incident. I had never felt so ashamed and violated. From this experience, I learned that the world doesn't give a damn about you or anyone else.

LOOKING FOR MY ROSE DURING DAWN – SAFARI

It was hard looking for the woman of my dreams. I went through so much. After years of dating men and then years of dating women, I realized that gender really didn't matter in affairs of the heart. I also learned that men and women can be dogs, liars, cheaters and they all creep. Most are on the down low, married with children, and creeping with other women. I swear I spent three years alone after a bad break up. I went through a true mental crisis. I partied, drank and just did any and every wild thing I could imagine. I was just sick of it all. Relationships and just dealing with other people was just not for me. I just wanted to have fun and I showed it in the wildest way. I dressed sexy and I swiveled my hips. I always had big hair, lotsa make up on my face and the highest heels ever. I have always been known as that Florida "Hot girl." And, I knew it. I had so much fun. I kept meeting women who wanted to fall in love with me which made life a little harder. After awhile, I decided to just venture out and meet people on the Internet and all kinds of ways to make it interesting. For a while, Internet dating was a lot of fun, but then I grew tired of the huge long distance bills and the many expensive trips. I realized after dating two women from New York, that out of state dating was the pits and I wanted a woman here and now. I met this girl named Shane at my college. I thought, "Wow." She is hot and single. Shane asked me into her office. I looked like a street bum. Shane invited me on a date to the movies. I was so excited. I got my hair done, nails done and my best hot girl clothes. I swear I spent so much on myself that day that I would have to work for at least a month to pay the bills. Well on the date Shane just seemed so sweet laid back and just sexy. Her lips were like pink tulips wrapped in cotton candy. I wanted to kiss them. At dinner Shane and I ordered dinner and drinks. We struck up a conversation and somehow we got to the subject of being single. Shane looked at me and said. "Oh I am not single." "What would make you think that?" I just remember yelling out the biggest "WHAT?" I was royally pissed. I had sat in the salon for at least four hours. Spent another hour and a half for my nails and eyebrows and put on my best clothes for this clown? I was so mad. I started shaking! I told Shane I wanted my food to go and I wanted to go home. Shane was such a heartless jerk. She apologized, but she sat there with a smile the whole time. She drove me home. I sat in the passenger seat and I cried my eyes out the whole way home. I was so hurt and humiliated. I got out of Shane's car and just walked in the house with my head hanging low.

DOING IT TILL DAWN

SAFARI

I knew that finding the woman of my dreams was going to be no easy task. I searched for a woman for at least a year and a half. Through, all the blind date hook ups, I meet some of the craziest women on earth. I met this girl from Jacksonville named Dawn. Dawn was a chain smoking weed puffer Social Worker, who would take peoples children because they had weed in the house. I had never in my life tried marijuana and I said, "Well what the heck." I tried it a few times with Dawn and it just made me fall asleep in the middle of sex. I slept really well. It was harmless. Well, one day Dawn was at work and I was super bored. I decided that I was going to drink warm leftover wine from the night before, alone while on the Internet. I soon became really bored. I wanted more excitement and Dawn was working a twelve-hour shift that day. So, I decided I would sneak and smoke the forbidden weed alone without Dawn. Dawn had warned me to never smoke without her and I thought "How stupid I am a grown woman and I don't need Dawn to help me smoke a pipe of weed." About an hour later, I was on the Internet typing crazy messages to my friends and just totally acting like a weirdo. Dawn called me and told me that she was coming to get me, and that I was going to hangout with her for the rest of the day. I wouldn't have to spend the whole day alone. Now that was a horrible idea. I sprayed the whole room over and over with air freshener and attempted to find an outfit to wear. Dawn came in less than ten minutes. I had never been high in my life. I didn't realize that I was walking in circles. I was not getting anything accomplished along with my jibber jabber mumbling. Finally, Dawn told me to get in the shower. And, that she would choose my clothes. When I finally got dressed and into the car I knew, I had pulled it off. Dawn didn't even notice that I was high as a kite, and boy did it feel good. Well that was until, the car started to move. I had not eaten all day and the wine in my stomach started to swim. All of a sudden my head started to spin out of control. I laid my seat back and thought I would be ok. All of a sudden, I busted out crying and I blurted out in a slurred dazed voice "I have a confession to make." "Dawn, I was bad." "I smoked the weed." She said "What?" I said, "I smoked the ganja weed." I started crying because it seemed like the world was spinning around faster and faster and faster. We arrived at a family's house and she told me to stay in the car because she was there to possibly take the children from the parents for the possession of marijuana. I was high as a kite in her car. I sat in that car for what seemed like hours and I vomited over and over again. Finally, the only thing I could remember was that my mother told me to do. When all else fails is to pray. I started praying and I asked the Lord to just make me fall asleep, so I wouldn't be sick anymore, and my head would stop spinning. This was weed? Hell, I never wanted to do this nutty thing again. Well just before I closed my eyes, I saw some children-playing hockey on the street. All of a sudden, I saw them skating towards the windshield at high speed and then just, as they were about to crash into the glass window. I screamed and passed out. When I came too, Dawn was in the car driving. I still had tears running down my face and she said, "I was crying in my sleep." Once again the car was moving and I began to vomit. Finally, when we got home, Dawn was so angry that she carried me in the house put me in the shower, gave me two white pills and then dressed me for bed. I woke up several hours later refreshed and glad that weed ride was over. As Dawn yelled at me, I happily slurped my chicken soup and hot tea while her oh so gay roommate Ronnie just shook his head and said "Umm Umm Ummm, honey you are just too much for me." Dawn ended up being a lying cheating woman and the sex with her was horrible anyway. I left Jacksonville. I caught her one time with her ex and I never went back. So my Journey continued for my Rose.

CHAPTER IV

HOMO EROTIC MISS ADDICTION 125TH STREET

By, Rose Sutra

HOW PYSCHO CAN A SISTA GET?

Homoerotic exotic neurotic robotic,

Strange world, strange girl, strange scene,

What does it all really mean?

See coming from the NYC, living in this world,

You gotta have big dreams, big dreams, big dreams...

That's what she told me, as I stood there on 125th street selling my poetry

cds.

Jus shooting the breeze, as she was vibe spittin' at me how she felt about

being a lesbian,

And how she was teased by her family, the ones closest to her!

As she poured out her heart to me, as she poured out her heart to me

And said, "I love women because they love me," I love my momma because she loved me first see!"

"So now I have grown to appreciate women that come in all shapes, sizes, race and colors.

"So I don't scriticize, and for becoming a lesbian and loving women I won't apologize."

She told me to me to look deep into her eyes, deep into her eyes, so I did, as each tear rolled down to her chin.

She said, "I have loved many women; I have had several interment relationships; but to be an outcast; shunned by my family that hurt me, that hurt me."

As we stood there on 125th street shooting the breeze, she said, "By the way Sis what's your name?"

"Oh I didn't tell you, I'm that famous poet they call Sista Flame booh, and guess what?"

She said, "What?"

And I am a lesbian too, shoooooooo, "word booh"

And I have been going through the same thing that you have been going through,

So don't be ashamed, it's just the players and haters trying to wreck your game,

But be who you are, love inner self.

We as lesbians know the hardness. We feel the softness...

As we stood there on 125th street vibin', feelin' na breeze, speakin' our peace;

She hugged me and said, "I'll see you again Sis along my journey, on this path, on this Harlem city street." As we raised arms, bumped fist, and said, "peace-peace."

(On any street any street corner)

As stood there and continued to yell poetry, poetry, poetry...

MISS ADDICTION

As I turned my head and glanced this lady in the corner, I call her MISS ADDICTION.

MISS ADDICTION, why so much friction?

Why so much rejection? Why so much frustration against your inner nation?

Why so much annihilation? Why does your personality and character have so much animation?

MISS ADDICTION, we come to build a nation and birth babies that are healthy to procreate our mighty generation.

MISS ADDICTION, as I ride through these neighborhoods, I see MISS ADDITION is rapping our neighbor hoodz, polluting our headz, People are strung out can't get out of the hood, so you tell me what's good?

MISS ADDITICTION, I 'm not scared of you, because I too have embraced you…

I have felt you. I have gone through you, and now look at me, look at me!

I am over.

MISS ADDICTION, I can now stand and tell those that don't know you to welcome you,

Because you are the addiction that we must all go through, you are the addition that we must all go through, you are the addition that we must all go through…

MISS ADDICTION, what's your addiction?

NOW HOW PSYCHO CAN A SISTA GET?

<u>JUST A FUCK!</u>

Fuck me, fuck me; fuck me was all she said,

So I did, as she laid there, I fucked her, fucked her, fucked her

Because that's all she wanted was a fuck a roll in the hay!

She didn't even know my name; but I knew hers.

Her name was love, but love wasn't ready for the truth and truth wasn't

Ready for us.

So I walked away with nothing, and she walked away with JUST A FUCK! NOW HOW PSYCHO CAN A SISTA GET?

LONG-TERM RELATIONSHIPS

By, Rose Sutra

Now that I was 25, I wanted more than just sex. I craved love, affection, togetherness, passion, and waking up to the same face every morning. I wanted a real relationship. You know, what Jody Watley was talking about, "I'm looking for a real love baby, a real love." I was now going to give love a chance. Genie was my first live in lover for five years. We had a lot in common and lots of fun together. I learned so much from her about my African Heritage, and spiritual realities. Genie was a book worm, very soft spoken, quiet, private, loved to travel, dance, and made sure home was taken care of first. Genie was one year older than me. She was five feet two inches, permed black hair to her shoulders, brown skinned, features like a black foot Indian, sensitive, a Pisces and very thin body. Sex with Genie I guess was all right. I was not really with here for the sex. I was with her because she fulfilled a need in my life at the time. My moms had passed so Genie was family to me and that's why I stayed so long with her. Don't get me wrong I loved Genie like friend and sister.

When you make a Pisces mad, they become sharks. Chile, I turned Genie into a shark. Yeah, I have always been the jealous type. Why? I have yet to this day found out why? But, any way we had our ups and downs. After two years of living together we stopped having sex, and we stopped going out together. The interment part of the relationship ended. She cheated on me. I have never cheated on her. When I found out I went off. I hit Genie first. Me raising my hand to her is what ended the relationship. We now had a relationship where we both paid rent together until I moved out. It took me a while to move out. I started seeing Rhonda will I was living with Genie. It was all good. We both were single and agreed to see other people.

RHONDA

I met Rhonda working for Prudential as a Mail Clerk in Nassau County Long Island. Rhonda was five foot seven, a Libra; her skin tone was blue black, short permed hair, very nice body, and dark brown eyes. At the time, I was looking for a new rap partner to work with. My DJ at the time told me about her. He gave me her phone number. I called her and we talked for about an hour. We both decided to set a date to meet up. When we met up, we clicked. She could rap her ass off. Rhonda was a lyricist. We started rehearsing together a lot. We ended recording a demo for a record label together, but the producer sat us both down and said to me "I could get you signed to Def Jam Records, but what are you going to do for me?" I answered, "Make good music, and kick out some banging lyrics." He told me to my face that is not enough, I want you to sleep with me." I told him no. And, that's where my association ended with him. He kept Rhonda's voice on the record, which was released over seas. Rhonda and I remained friends. Why wouldn't we? We were lovers at the time. What broke Rhonda and I up was that she did too much drugs, and she left my life for one month. Once she left. I saw a lot of things much more clearly. That's when I went back to college to finish my degree. Two months later, Rhonda pops up out of now where. She was waiting for me at my front door, when I had come home from school. I looked at her as if she were a ghost. I said, "What are you doing here?" Rhonda replied, "I came back." I said, "Came back to me for what?" Rhonda said, "You and me." I said, "There is no you and me, remember you left and went down South somewhere. "She replied, "Well I am back and I would like to pick up where we had left off. I said, "Well that is not going to happen, I have moved on." Rhonda acted like she did not hear me. She said, "Let's go get some smoke." I told her that, I did not do that anymore. I was back in school trying to finish my education. Besides Rhonda was doing much more that smoking marijuana. She was also smoking crack. That's why she probably didn't stay with Queen Latifah. Latifah from what I heard was in love with Rhonda. But Rhonda told me that she was too heavy set for her. To quote her, "She had too many rolls of fat." I told her no, I would not go with her anywhere. I kindly walked her to the bus stop and told her bye. I never saw her again.

LYNN

I saw this fine chic walking down the hill from City College located Up-Town Manhattan New York. She had long sandy- light brown/red hair, tight blue jeans, red cowboy hat and some red cowboy boots to match. I thought to myself she was hot. I followed her into the train station. She got on the A train to Brooklyn. So I hopped on the same train. I didn't have enough nerve to talk to her so I watched her get off the train and disappear. Until one year later, my wish had come true. Lynn had walked into Crazy Nanny's one night with the same exact outfit on. At the time I was on the dance floor with my Pat dancing. I turned around and nearly jumped out of my skin. I could not believe it. The angels answered my prayer. I tapped Pat on the shoulder and said, "There's that girl I was telling you about." Pat said, don't miss your chance this time, go and talk to her." So, I built up my confidence, walked over her and asked her if she had wanted to dance. She said, "Yes." We proceeded to dance. As we were dancing we talked and exchanged telephone numbers. She told me that she would call me the next morning. She had left with her friend.

The next morning, the phone had ringed. Genie gave me the phone, and said, "It's some lady." I picked up the phone. It was Lynn. We talked for about five minutes. We had set a dinner date at her house in Brooklyn that night. I was excited. I arrived at her house at eight o'clock that evening as she asked. She was dressed in long skirt and see through blouse. Home girl was the bomb. All I thought about was having sex. We sat in her living room and talked while dinner was cooking. She served cocktail drinks before dinner. Twenty minutes later, dinner was served. She had cooked a seafood dinner. The meal was very delicious. Once we were both done eating, we stood up and began to walk towards the living room. I through her up against the wall and started kissing her. She kissed me back. I started pulling off her cloths. She did not say stop. She said let's go into my bedroom. Once in the bedroom, I laid her down on the bed and started touching her body from bottom to top. As I worked my way up to her breast, one breast was nice and soft and the other one was hard as a rock. I stopped in the middle of lovemaking, and asked her what is this that I am feeling. She told me that she had silicon implants. I tripped out. One, I did not know anything about silicon tities. This just broke the mood for me. I thought she was some type of alien. We did not make love that; we talked all night until we fell a sleep in each other arms. I got up the next morning and went home. I let a couple of days pass and decided to call her back. I really liked her despite her medical problem. We started dating after I begged for a second date. This is where the drama begins.

Danger sign number one, danger sign number two, danger sign number, aw fuck it. I am sitting in prison, cell block 23 on danger sign number three. Stupid me, I should have put my name on the lease. What was I thinking? At the time I was not smoking or drinking. However, I found out the hard way about her lies and her cheating ways. Look ladies learn from my lesson. If she has silicon tities leave her alone. Once a woman goes under the knife for bigger breasts it's over mentally for her. Stupid me, it was all about he breast implants and doctorate degree. Stupid me, money that I could have used to finish my college degree, buy a nicer car, and a house, instead I gave all my money to miss silicon queen. Lynn was fourteen years older than I. She was a Libra. Danger sign number three, Lynn had crossed the line with me when she messed with my finances and swindled me. Now ladies when you use others peoples money for your personal gain without them knowing, you are setting yourself up for a rude awakening. But, I guess it was the sandy blonde, curly weave, red cowboy boots, hat and blue jeans that got me? How could I be so blind? I spent twenty-two days in prison on a B4 mister meaner for unlawful imprisonment, for loving another female.

Lynn told me that her rent was $1000 a month. I paid $450 and I thought she would pay the other half. As soon as I moved in, she moved a foreign exchange student in her son's room. She had her son stay with one her friends for two months. He paid $450 also. That added up to $900, which meant Lynn was paying $100. I agreed to this transaction verbally, but I was not happy that I had to live with another man in the house. I thought it was going to be her son David, Lynn and myself, as a family. One morning, as I walked as I was sitting in the living room, a piece of paper was pushed under the door. I picked up the envelope. I opened it. It was a rent receipt, stated that her rent was only $250 every month. Lynn had been living in this co-op for fourteen years. As I read this document. I was heated. I felt that I had been swindled. I waited until she arrived home that night. Once she had came and got comfortable. I took the keys out the door, and hid them. Lynn was going to hear I felt about this entire situation. I asked her who were the other women that she was cheating with? I asked her why did she lie to me about the cost of her rent? She sat there surprised that I found out. At this point, I knew that I had been financially used. Being that I am an Aries, I went off. Lynn lived on the 18th floor. I had all types of evil thoughts flowing in my mind. I said to Lynn, "I should throw your ass over the terrace for what you have done." That scared the shit out of her. I was going to terrorize this bitch for using me. I pulled the phone cords from the wall, so she could not make any phone calls. The only conversation she would have would be with me that entire night. I told her that I knew everything that was going on. I told her that I wanted my money back. I knew, I would never get that back. I never hit her. I verbally terrorized her. She was going to feel my pain. I held Lynn hostage all night. I called her every last name in the book that night. I should have never worked roots to have Lynn in my life. I should have never burned a candle to get her and continued to burn candles to keep her. I messed my own life up at this point. Ladies take it from me, once it's over it's over. Don't ever look back, or you will be that pillar of salt. I was in love her. I asked why would she do this? She had no answer. She continuously was trying to find ways of escaping her own house, but she failed. She even tried to gently talk her way out. Nothing worked. We both did not get any sleep that night.

The next morning, I decided to leave. I gave her the keys to her apartment back and I went back to Genie's house. I had taken three days off from work to recuperate. While I was laying on the couch in the living room, I heard a knock at the door. Something told me not to answer the door. But, stupid me did. Why did I do that? When I said, "Who is it?" The voice on the other side of the door said, "It is detective Robertson with New York City Police Department, open the door." I had no choice but to open the door. Once I had opened the door. The Officer asked was I Rose Sutra? I replied, "Yes." The officer told me that I was under arrest. I had never in my life been arrested. Officer Robertson asked where was I at for the past three days? I told him in the house. I had thought to myself, lucky I had given away my two marijuana plants a couple days ago. I may have gone to prison for growing marijuana. The officer told me to get dressed. I did as he asked. I was escorted out of my house in handcuffs.

When we arrived at the police station. I was taken in small room. The officer told me sit down. The officer told me why I was brought to the police station. The officer also told me that I had the right to have her arrested too. Not knowing my rights at the time I declined. From that point I was put processed through the system as a criminal. I spent twenty-two days in prison for this bitch. This was not love, I had thought to myself. Yet, I was still in love with her. I was in a four-year relationship with this woman. I said to myself, "How could she?" I had spent 21 days in solitary confinement because I refused to take a Pap smear test. My twenty-second day, I spent in population in the lesbian section of the prison. Boy was I hating that. I had to spend on full day and night with a bunch of thirsty lesbian women. I was subjected to playing a card game with a bunch of dykes. You talking about scared straight. I was shitting bricks. I just knew I was the pussy to be served. Boy, were they some characters. After the card game, the ringmaster, head leader within that cell bloc, she took me on a tour and introduced me to the women in that cellblock. Princess must have really thought that I was staying for a while. Then Princess took me back to her cell and showed me who had the most money and most pull in that section. It was she. Her cell was hooked up. I hung out with her for a little while longer and she escorted me back to my cell. I was so happy to be back in my cell and away from those vulture's. As soon as she left and I closed my door. I dropped to my knees, began crying and started to prayer, that I be released from this nightmare.

The next morning, I was late getting up. I had missed breakfast. I went to take a shower. Guess who was in the shower? It was Princess. I was nude.

Princess looked me up and down and said, "What's a pretty girl like you doing here?" "You look like, you don't belong here." "What did you do?" I put my cloths on so fast and tried to avoid any of her questions. Fuck that, I was not going to get a stick shoved up my ass in the shower. I flew out that shower and back to my cell. I refused to eat or come out of my cell. For the next half-hour, I began to prayer. I heard my name Rose Sutra over the loud speakers stating that I was released. I jumped off my knees; packed what little things I had and headed for the front gate to be escorted to out. This was one of the happiest days of my life. I vowed not to go back to prison.

I was back home. Genie was happy to see me. Genie said to me, "If I were you, I would never talk to Lynn again." I should have taken Genie's advice, but I didn't. I was still in love with Lynn and she was still in love with me too. Lynn Had called me the next day. She must have known I was released. Lynn told me how sorry she was, and how much she had missed me. Stupid me I moved back in with her. We broke up six months later. She continued to cheat. I finally kissed that relationship goodbye.

After that traumatizing dysfunctional relationship I joined the Army National Guard. That was a big mistake. I was trying to get away from the drama, I ran into more drama. I thought I could be G.I. Jane and kill people for a living, because I was so angry. That did not work out either.

After three months, I left the Army. When I got back to New York, I vowed to stay away from women and relationships. I was single and loving it. I was twenty-nine. I continued with my education in college and outside of college. I pursued my music with a passion and vengeance. I took three years of from college to produce six spoken word poetry cds, three poetry chapbooks and started my own small business for my self-produced products. I wrote about my life in my music and poetry. It was all about my talent. I was doing shows, vending at events, and performing at different locations. I also worked for an underground radio station in Long Island New York. I produced thirty two-minute shows called the "Third Eye Teaching." I was also hosting my own poetry shows and paying poets to perform. I was getting several write-ups in newspapers and Internet articles for my poetry and stories. I opened up the second Million Youth March with an Opening Prayer from the Shrine Of Ma'at. This was to help stop the violence. I was finally focusing.

I was having lots of fun until 911, the World Trade Towers blew up. After 911 everybody in New York City was mentally meshed up. I was still in college trying to finish my education. My dread locs had grew down to my butt. I was a strict vegetarian. I was in search for my higher self. So I started to take spiritual classes with Queen Afua, The Shrine Of Maat' (EL Ashera), Dr. Rev. Phil Valentine, Francis Hewitt, Dr. Leonard Jeffries, Dr. Smalls Dr. Ben, Doc Bongo, Lady Prema, etc. I became a Buddhist. I studied Yoruba, Zen, voodoo, and black magic. I spent two years in school to become a non-denominational Certified Ordained Minister (Sanctuary of the Beloved), located upstate New York. So I took another two years off from women to find out who was Rose Sutra? I have learned thus far, to get far in life you have to let go of the old to allow the new in. That's what I did. I packed my belongings, and moved to Orlando Florida.

.SAFARI

By Rose

I met Safari at a poetry reading at the Grand Bohemian Hotel hosted by 94.5 F.M. radio station in downtown Orlando Florida. Jade and her girlfriend Angela introduced me to her. When Jade introduced me to Safari, I thought she was really attractive. Safari had a nice ass, a curly weave, a nice body, dark brown eyes, dark skinned, a Sagittarian and a nice personality. She was about one inch taller than me. But she was out with another woman that night, which, I thought was her girlfriend. I did not ask her for her telephone number that night. Jade and Angela had driven home that night after the show.

The next day, I was invited to a woman's discussion group this café in Pine Hills also known as Crime Hills! I also was asked to perform that day. As I was sitting with Jade and Angela, in walked Safari, breasts bouncing, and ass jiggling. I said to myself, "That is the fine sister from last night. I asked Jade was Safari single? Jade replied, "She is very single, go and talk to her." I waited until intermission to chat with her.

During intermission, I walked over to Safari and said, "My name is Rose." She said, "Nice to met you; I am going out to my car for a minute." I asked her, "Can I accompany you?" Safari said, "Sure." We talked as we walked. She opened up her car door and popped the lock, so I could get in.

We proceeded to talk a little more. I told her that she was very attractive. I wrote my phone number on a piece of paper and stated, "That I would like to get to know her in every way." I passed her the note and asked Safari could I kiss her? She told me no. I said, "Oh come on, one little kiss on the cheek." Safari said no again. I said "Ok." I got out her car and told her I would see her back inside. She did not know that I was performing that night. When I took the stage, she was surprised. After I performed I knew Safari would be mine.

The group meeting continued after I performed. I said so many interesting off the wall things that night, Safari blurted out to everyone, "That Rose is making me hot, and my heart is beating so fast." From that point on I knew she would be driving me home tonight. I did not have a car at the time.

Ronnie walks in the Café. Ronnie is about five foot five, dread locs, and not cute to me. I am a soft butch with fem features. Ronnie walked up to me and said, "I drove all the way from work to drive you home tonight." I replied, "Safari is driving me home." I made Ronnie feel low, and Safari looked at me, like no you didn't volunteer me, and my car! I looked at her and said, "Thank you, and smiled." Yeah, I was a bit pushy, but I knew what I wanted. I craved Safari.

The meeting ended. Both Safari and I left. She had driven me home. We sat out front for a while in her car talking. She originally was going to be a one-nightstand, but we ended up dating. At the time, I was living with my aunt Joan. Safari and I had gone out to club one night and was drinking shots. We both were very drunk. I knew once she drove me home, she was unable to drive anymore. I had invited her to spend the night. Once she came in. My intentions were to go to sleep, and get her out before my aunt woke up. But, when Safari pulled down her pants, I could not resist wanting eat her vagina. I didn't have sex in a while. I was hungry and thirsty. I started kissing her twat. The next thing I knew, we were in the bed having sex. I was too drunk to recall anything. When I woke up Safari was laying next me.

The next morning, my aunt left to go run errands. I knew I should have told Safari to leave. Instead, I made her breakfast. I had made her an egg omelet stuffed with corn. My aunt came back in, and called me into the living room. She totally embarrassed me in front of Safari. My aunt Joan told me that I had disrespected her home and that I had to find another place to live. Safari had to leave, and I had to find another place to live quickly. The power of the pussy will get you in trouble.

LONG-TERM RELATIONSHIPS

SAFARI

ALEERA

Six of my relatives had died within a six-month span. I was on the brink of insanity and drinking heavily. Everyday I felt like I was going to snap. I was living alone for the first time in my life. I hated my job, but I loved my apartment. I didn't miss home with my parents and I would've worked twenty jobs to stay far away from their home of chaos. Drinking and sleeping became my best friends. I met Aleera one night at the club in the parking lot. I was drunk and seeing double. The funny thing is that I was actually checking her super fine friend, Ronnie. Ronnie was a hot dark chocolicious sexy girl who was also drunk. She pissed on herself. She started crying in front of everybody and saying how bad she wanted her mommy. Trust me it wasn't cute, but she was! The next thing I knew, I was in a relationship with Aleera. Our relationship ended up being a rebound relationship that, I really didn't need. But, I was such a mess after Savvon, that I just needed another woman's arms to rock me. I made the mistake of giving Aleera a key to my apartment. She practically moved in to my place, ran up my phone bill, and I would wake to her standing over my bed staring at me. She was really creepy and honestly not my type. Aleera convinced me that living together was a necessary part of being a lesbian and that it would be impossible for us to be together. If we did live together, she promised to help me Finish College She told me I would on easy street while living with her. This was the biggest mistake I had ever made. After this tragedy with Aleera I would never be the same again. I dated Aleera for over a year and everything boiled down to a phone call from an ex best friend of hers named Jill. Jill and Aleera were no longer friends due to past conflicts and drama. Jill called me to tell me, that Aleera and Samantha lied about their whereabouts. Aleera told me she was on a business trip in Georgia and Sam said, "She was redecorating her new house that she had just bought." It turns about the Aleera and Sam was together in another city in Florida. Them lying hoes! On a three-way phone call, they admitted to Jill that they had made love all weekend. Neither of them had any remorse and didn't show any sign of dignity or respect on my part. I even found out that Sam had been driving my car. Aleera had been sleeping with Sam for months behind my back. I was furious! I took it upon myself to call Sam's girlfriend and inform her of the vicious and dirty antics of her precious Samantha. Sam had been sleeping with several other women around town and women in other states. When Sam and Aleera arrived in Orlando, they met with Sam's girlfriend. Waiting with anger and incriminating photos that I provided as proof. Samantha cursed my name, but of course those two were caught red handed. The sad part of the situation is that Aleera's best friend Ronnie knew all along that they were fooling around and kept it hidden. I was hur, confused and stark raving mad. I cried for what seemed like a lifetime and attempted to take my life by swalling pills and alcohol. But, I guess it just wasn't my time. For about six months I stayed in my room. I cried, prayed, bathed and slept my life away. It wasn't, because I had been in love with Aleera. Actually, I had no attraction to her at all. I just couldn't believe that two people could be so evil, thoughtless and heartless towards another human being. I will never forget being told by Aleera that would have to move to the guest bedroom and Sam was moving in the master bedroom with her, and sleeping on my side of the bed. It was a devastating and felt like a million slaps across my face. I just wanted to die. I was so humiliated. After about seven months of total isolation, I got a job at a local bank. I was angry and was determined to seek revenge on the women who ruined my entire life. It took me about two years to finally move on. I was so hurt to find out that those two bitches from hell got married. And, of course I wasn't invited. The entire lesbian community was invited and I was left to find out the sickening details through gossip. Although I dismissed this tragic affair from my heart I never forgave those two for what they did to me. I still have a deep hatred in my heart for the evil deeds that ripped my heart in two. The lesbian life seems to be full of these lovely heartbreaking surprises. My wounds began to heal. My hatred became a distant memory. I found out some news through the town gossip that knocked me off my feet.

ALEERA- FLASH FORWARD

By Safari

So here I am, with my mouth wide open and the sad part is that I am pissed off. My face is heated and I feel tears welling up in my eyes. I don't know why I am reacting this way to a new beautiful life that was brought into this world. You know people are some shady creatures. I mean who would believe that my ex girlfriend who cheated on me would have a baby? This is the same woman who cheated on me and threw me into a state of depression, tried to rob me of all my money and looked like a man, yet acted like a woman? The thing that really pissed me off is that not only did the ruthless hussies try to ruin my life for no reason at all but also her and her evil girlfriend didn't care that they ruined my life and changed me forever. Those good for nothing she-devils never invited me to their wedding nor to their baby shower. Hell, I didn't even know my ex Aleera was pregnant. The kicker is that Aleera's best friend never breathed a word to me and she knew all along all the dirty deeds her best buddy was doing to me. I tell you people from Texas are now looked upon as enemies in my eyes because several Texans have tried to destroy me including she devil one and two. Here I am again alone and thinking that they could've called, sent a postcard or even a smoke signal somebody could've told me something. The sad and jacked up part of the whole thing is that my so-called friends along with everyone else in town knew about the baby except me. If I have not learned anything about life, I have learned that the world of lesbianism is a roller coaster ride from hell. Sometimes, I want to get off this horrific ride from Hades and just have peace in my heart in mind. I have learned that this world of gayness is like a roach motel, once you check in you can't check out! Being a gay woman has its beautiful moments, like when you and your girl walk hand and hand on the beach or you cuddle to watch a movie together. Sometimes, I wonder, if I were a straight woman what would it be like? What would it have been like to marry a man and have children? Would I have been happier? Sometimes, I feel so sad because I know that in this society being gay, black and a female is a triple threat. Life is already hard. Why would anyone choose this lifestyle? Why did I choose this lifestyle? I call myself a choosebian. I am the type of lesbian that chose to be in this lifestyle. Hence, the name choosebian or choose-to-be in. Sometimes, I wish to unclose the lesbian life but being a wife to a man would be torture. I go back and forth in my mind questioning my sexuality. I never get a solid answer in my heart or mind. Sex with men was a selfish love for themselves. I always felt like I was nothing more than a hole to stick their penis into. That was not my idea of fun. Men are selfish lovers. Once they get their ultimate thrills you are left high, dry and orgasm less. As far as the lesbian world, I hear people say, "Gay is wrong and it isn't natural or I was born this way." I think that some gay women choose to be gay (which I call choosebians) based on bad experiences with men and others. I think this is a preference and some were just born to be gay. It does not matter how you entered this lifestyle. Sometimes you feel like you will be trapped forever in its madness. Sometimes, I wish I could get a one way ticket out of this hell! This nightmarish trip is like a reoccurring bad dream. I try to find hope and happiness. Maybe in time I will, but as for now, I want to get off at the next train stop and run like hell!

TARRICK

I stayed single for two years. I decided that it was time to date again. I was set up with this girl named Tarrick She was so fine! Tarrick was about five foot eleven five light brown skin with a muscular build. She was a professional volleyball player. I swear, she was a real man because she used to wear a sista out in bed. This girl dressed like a man and worked a strap on dildo better than any man I had ever been with. I remember Tarrick did something so strange one night while we were having sex. All of a sudden, I heard this noise that sounded like a spigot and her vagina started sqirting out liquid just like a water hose. I had never seen anything like this in my life. It had a funky smell. It looked as if someone had dumped a bucket of water over my head. I found out years later that this was called female ejaculation. I just called it nasty! The sex with Tarrick was wonderful. She was so strong and could make me howl louder than any hyiena south of the Mississippi. Most of our time that we spent together, we were drunk. We made love drunk always. I used to drink so much around Tarrick just to cope with the mental abuse and control that she had over me. Tarrick used to pee on herself every time she was drunk. Once, I was in the bed with her and I was lying across her backside, when I heard this familiar noise and I woke to her pissing on me. She was still sleeping, while pissing all over my brand new lingerie that I purchased. I was very upset with Tarrick. I started dragging her into the bathroom stripping her naked and checking on her periodically. Tarrick was insane. She had witnessed the murder of her mother when she was ten years old. I guess this is what made her insanely jealous and crazy. She would call me millions of times and accuse me of cheating all of the time. I felt like a prisoner with great sex. When Tarrick was naked she looked like a man. She had no breasts and just looked mannish all over. Tarrick had an 8-year-old son named King. She swore King had no idea that she was a lesbian. But, I knew he was a smart boy. I loved King so much, but his mother was from hell. Tarrick was the stingiest woman on the planet. Tarrick was twenty-nine years old. She looked about forty-three, because all of her drinking and smoking over the years. I always wondered how a dike butch like her could get pregnant by a man? Tarrick told me that her son had been conceived when she was high. She was trying to get free drugs from the drug man. She slept with him and got pregnant. Tarrick treated me like a dog. She made me bring my own food, water and always treated me bad.

One Christmas, Tarrick had the nerve to wrap up a bar of soap and the cheapest ring, I had ever seen, and gave it to me. The ring was so cheap and it looked like it came out of a bubble gum machine! Tarrick was extremely jealous and swore I was always cheating. One day, Tarrick threw a frying pan at my head. I ducked and the glass window behind me broke into a million pieces. She found out that I had told one of her friends about how she abused me and she was embarrassed. After a horrible day of fighting I broke it off with Tarrick. I was sick of her abuse, smoking, drinking and pissing in the bed every time she was drunk. That entire night I stayed up drunk yet in a trance like state praying to God and my deceased granny Safffie. I cried all night and prayed that God would make the devil release me from this hell and finally the next day my misery was over and Tarrick was on my out list. Of course Tarrick was not going to let me go without a fight, but she finally gave up with my brother stepped in and I ignored all threats and promises of eternal ruin that she promised me. I still see Tarrick around town and we have a hate hello kind of relationship. I keep my distance and she just acts like she doesn't know me. I miss King, but I hear he is a grown man and very successful. I hope he never forgot me. I remember secretly wishing that he were my son He was so much fun and the coolest kid I knew.

ROSE TAKES SAFARI

SAFARI

Her name was Rose. When I met Rose, I didn't think anything about her, but apparently she had eyes for me. I didn't plan on seeing Rose again after that night. A few days later, I reluctantly went to a lesbian group chat and there was Rose. I was not impressed by Rose Actually, I ignored her most of the meeting. Finally, I said something and Rose decided that she wanted to go against what I had said. I was heated. As I began to speak to her, I experienced the strangest hot flashes throughout my body. All of a sudden I said out loud "Did you know that when you speak you emit so much energy"? "My goodness you are making me sweat!" I was so embarrassed. Everyone began laughing. When we had a break, I headed for the door to try to make a phone call to Martina. I was going to invite her to the meeting. Just as I reached the door Rose stopped me and said, " I hear you are single." I said, "Yes, that is correct." Rose asked me if she could give me her number. She scribbled her name on a piece of paper that said, "I would like to get to know you in every way." I quickly thanked Rose and tried to walk away. Rose followed me to the car, got in, and tried to kiss me. I was not feeling this crazy chick. She even volunteered me to take her home. I was not very happy, but I thought I would be nice. I took her home. After a few weeks of us talking by phone and hanging out for our late night back seat of the car chats. I finally realized that Rose was kind of nice. I will never forget the night I invited Rose out to the club. She drank these shots called Red headed sluts. The next thing I knew, we were in her aunt's house having sex. I kept trying to keep Rose quiet, but she kept yelling out "I love pussy, oh I love pussy strap on dildo dicks and short skirts." I was certain that her aunt had heard us. Rose didn't seem to care.

The next day Rose's aunt apparently had heard the loud sex and she kicked Rose out. Rose moved from her aunt's house to a hotel then to another hotel. This second hotel was from hell. The neighbor was a prostitute with four children. She was constantly having sex with her Johns, while her children were at school. Rose lived in the hotel for five months. Our relationship grew and grew, but her jealously soon made the relationship hell. I wanted to leave many times. Rose is a sexy caramel skinned beauty, which has the hottest body. I still can remember her performing her spoken word poetry. I remember her slithering like a snake across the stage and then casually pulling up her shirt to expose the flatted stomach I had ever seen. Rose and I had so many problems despite our time growing together that we decided to go to a tarot card reader. The tarot card reader was on the mark with our relationship. She told us that we had experienced a lot of turmoil. We were soul mates. After visiting the tarot card reader Rose began to improve and change from a jealous woman to someone more understanding and caring. Finally, I had found the woman that I wanted to spend my life with after all the trials and tribulations; I had been through in my life. Rose was my future wife. When I woke the morning after our anniversary in the arms of my sweet Rose, I finally, was at peace with a woman who loved me. I loved her despite all of the problems. We were two happy lesbians in love and proud to be gay. The next day we went to Gay Days in Orlando Florida and I fell in love with Rose all over again as I watched her slither that sexy body that I fell in love with many years ago. I became hot with passion, knowing that when we got home, we were going to make love till the sun came up.

PART TWO: LEZORY FILES

Discipline…Patience…Self-control…

By, Rose Sutra

Discipline…Patience…Self-control…

Follow these rules and you will reach your goals.

Discipline…Patience…Self-control…

No backsliding on the road.

Discipline…Patience…Self-control…

Always look forward with a positive flow.

Discipline…Patience…Self-control…

Stick to your path, cause God knows

Discipline…Patience…Self-control…

Ask, and you shall receive all the riches that you need.

Discipline...Patience...Self-control...

You got to keep striving.

Stay strong....

You got to keep striving.

Stay strong....

FLASHBACK TO THE TIMES WE HAD

By, Safari

As Rose and I sit in the backseat of my car massaging each another's feet
and talking well into day break. I have flashbacks to all the times that I
had, good and bad. The flashbacks were not about my sweet; caramel
colored luscious lipped almond-eyed Rose. I was flashing back to the
WNBA hot summer. This super fine light skinned studdish, boyish player
with eyes like heaven and corn rowed hair "umm umm" she was fine. My
friends and I met this ball player one night after a game. My friend Cori,
Lynette and I decided was going be the next WNBA stalkers. Ok, we just
wanted to hug up with a player or two all in good fun no harm done to
anyone. Well, I can tell you it was a summer full of fun. I will never forget
the grand ole time that we had. The entire population of lesbians in our
town was in love with the WNBA players. Our biggest dream was to meet
a player and to be their one and only wifey. This particular night was our
lucky night. After the game, there were at least 10-15 carloads of hungry
lesbians followed the WNBA players at full speed back to their hotel. I
would say at least half of the lesbian stalkers didn't make it through the
front door or make it pass security. Cori and Lynette had the master plan.
Since, I was the skinny cute one, I had to flirt with the security guard to
get us in. After a little T-N-T action, we were in, and then the hunt was
on! We went to the bar and tried to bribe the bartenders to tell us where

the players were. It took an hour and about seventy-five dollars for us to find out that the players may be in a rooftop pool. Lynette, Cori and I casually strolled over to the elevator trying to not look too suspicious. Damn! There was that pesky security guard. I just pulled up my skirt and showed him a little leg. Then I laid a big fat kiss on old wrinkles forehead and with my cutest baby girl voice I whispered, "Now, I know you are going to tell me where the basketball players are right cutie?" That security guard was like a squawking jaybird with no teeth and about three strands of hair. He said, "They may or may not be on the fifth floor but you didn't hear that from me, then he winked." I winked my eye and blew another kiss at this funny looking old man, and we were off like a flash. Finally, after about two hours of searching we found the room where all the players were sitting, watching TV and having a good time. We had one small problem. Who would knock on the door? After debating for a while we decided to move in for a closer look. So we got on our hands and crawled past the window where the players were sitting. We peeked through the window and there they were. Fine, tall, sexy and best of all basketball players. Then all of a sudden we saw one of the ugliest player in the WNBA come out of the room as we were peeking out from around the corner contemplating our next move of shame. Lynetta all of a sudden got brave and ran out of the corner and asked the play Mistee Templeton if she could get our favorite player K Rockah she agreed. We were the happiest girls in the land. We waited for Mistee for at least thirty minutes.

As, I was talking at a million miles a minute about what I was going to say to the fine sexy K Rockah my friends just froze. I thought maybe a ghost or a grizzly bear had appeared. As I turned around, I nearly fainted there she was K Rockah was in the house. She was a let down. On the court she was so tall and so gorgeous and sexy but in person she was short sweet barefoot and eating apiece of chicken. How incredibly ghetto! K. Rockah talked and talked for about ten minutes then Lynette stopped the conversation and ended our happy moment. K. Rockah kissed each one of us on our cheeks and disappeared like a dream into the room of cackling chickens also known as WNBA players. When she was out of sight we all pretended to faint. I would never wash my face again.

KANSAS

As, I sit in the park and snuggle was with my aim, I flashed back to another woman who I thought was going to finally be the love of my life. Her nickname was Kansas. Kansas was this cute blue-black stud muffin boyish girl who was just sexy to the bone. I met Kansas through a friend and when I inquired about her one day she and I hooked up and hung out. Kansas seemed to be fun, but she was part of a taboo world that I was not so sure I wanted to get involved with. Kansas was 20 years old a full of energy. At first I wanted no part of Kansas because I felt like dealing with a baby could be more that just drama. I was 28 years old and a lot wiser but something about this girl sparked my bright lights. Needless to say, I gave Kansas a chance and we had the shortest relationship in recorded history. I swear, we dated for about a week and Kansas kicked me to the curb! One night Kansas and some friends of ours decided that we were all going out to a local club together. It was Valentines Day and I had to wear that special red Valentines dress with matching heels and fishnet stockings. I was fly and I knew it. As the night went on, I remember telling one of my friends that my drink tasted a little funny. I had the strangest tasting long island iced tea. I drank it and ordered another. I only took a few sips of my second drink and Kansas told me she was ready to leave. Kansas hopped in the car and we were taking one of her friend's homes and then I blacked out. The next thing I knew is that I woke up at Kansas's house alone. I had on nothing but a g-string and all my clothes were missing. I was throwing up in a bucket. Someone had dropped something in my drink. I think they used the date rape drug. I was terrified just thinking about what may have happened to me. There was no one else around and I didn't remember anything. I was scared. At first I didn't know what the hell to do or what happened to me but then Kansas's roommate Lori came out and told me that I had been very ill all night long. The very same day Kansas came home from work and dumped me! I couldn't believe that someone drugged me and I got dumped for it? Kansas refused to believe me and broke up with me that day. She called me a drunk and just wrote me out of her life. I was so hurt. I knew I only drank one and a half drinks. I knew I had not been intoxicated. I thought to myself "Where is all of the compassion that I thought women would have for one another?" I stopped all communication with Kansas until one day she called me and we straightened out all of the drama that went down between us and cleared the air. I hear these days Kansas is a fugitive and running from the police. I saw her at a party recently and she looked bad. She looked like she has been using lots of drugs and looked much older than her 22 years. With Kansas, I am more than happy that she and I parted ways because in the long run she was trouble with a capitol "T." To this day I wonder if Kansas or one of her friends dropped the date rape drug in my drink and was I raped? Today that is still a mystery to me and I fear that unauthorized pictures or video may come out with me being raped by a gang of girls. Kansas is known for hanging around thugs and criminals. You never know about a woman like that. Lesbianism isn't all that it is cracked up to be. You are constantly subjected to hateful acts by women and must always watch your back or else somebody is going to take you out.

So, here I am mouth wide open and the sad part is that I am pissed off. My face is heated and I feel tears welling up in my eyes. I don't know why I am reacting this way to a new beautiful life that was brought into this world. You know people are some shady creatures. I mean who would believe that my ex girlfriend who cheated on me would have a baby. This is the same woman who cheated on me and threw me into a state of depression, tried to rob me of all my money and looked like a man. The thing that really pissed me off is that not only did the ruthless hussies try to ruin my life for no reason at all but also her and her evil girlfriend didn't care that they ruined my life and changed me forever. Those good for nothing she-devils never invited me to their wedding nor to their baby shower. Hell, I didn't even know my ex Aileen was pregnant. The kicker is that Aileen's best friend never breathed a word to me. I tell you people from Texas are now looked upon as enemies in my eyes because several Texans have tried to destroy me including she devil one and two. So here I am again alone and thinking that they could've called, sent a postcard or even a smoke signal somebody could've told me something. The sad and jacked up part of the whole thing is that my so-called friends along with everyone else in town knew about the baby except me. If I have not learned anything about life I have learned that the world of lesbianism is a roller coaster from hell. Sometimes I want to get off this horrific ride from Hades and just have peace in my heart in mind. I have learned that this world of gayness is like a roach motel, once you check in you can't check out. Being a gay woman has its beautiful moments like when you and your girl walk hand and hand on the beach or you cuddle to watch a movie together. Sometimes, I wonder if I were a straight woman what would it be like? What would it have been like to marry a man and have children? Would I have been happier? Sometimes I feel so sad because I know that in this society being gay, black and a female is a triple threat. Life is already hard so why would anyone choose this lifestyle? Why did I choose this lifestyle? I go back and forth in my mind questioning my sexuality but I never get a solid answer in my heart or mind. Sex with men was a selfish love for themselves. I always felt like I was nothing more than a hole to stick their penis into and that was not my idea of fun. Men are selfish lovers and as long as the get their ultimate thrills you are left high and dry and orgasm less. As far as the lesbian world, I hear people say gay is wrong and it isn't natural or I was born this way. I think that some gay women choose to be gay based on bad experiences with men and others this is a preference and some were just born to be gay. It does not matter though how you entered this lifestyle because you will be trapped forever in its madness. Sometimes I wish I could get a one way ticket out of this hell but somehow this nightmarish trip is like a reoccurring bad dream. Within it I try to find hope and happiness and maybe in time I will but as of today I want to get off at the next stop and run like hell

ROSE AND ME
By Safari

The apple of my eye, the sweetness in my heart and the biggest pain in my butt! With Rose life has been an emotional, jealousy-reddened road to hell. When I met Rose at first to me, she was like an annoying mosquito buzzing around your ears just searching for a spot to suck your blood to quench her thirst. For some reason over time Rose started to grow on me.

150

She was an exotic, erotic poet who was full of mystery. I loved the rest of her qualities but her lies and jealousy were too much to bear. Her ex's scarred her life forever and for their mistakes and mistreatment to Rose, I suffered. I can remember that I thought Rose was a fugitive or a secret agent because she hid things from me and was super secretive about everything. Rose would never tell me much that was the truth. The truth and lies became so mixed up that I didn't know what to believe. Miss thing had issues. When Rose got kicked out of her aunt's home because of our late night of drunken sex, I was there for her. When her two super faggot roommates from Mars, Roy and Jake kicked Rose out in the middle of Florida's third hurricane in three weeks. I was there for Rose. Rose began accusing me of cheating on her with every woman in Florida and the terrible part was that I had been faithful to her the whole time. Honestly, I became mentally and physically tired. I felt like I was being thrown around in a tsunami and fighting for my life on a daily basis and I was losing the fight. For months I contemplated leaving Rose. Just saying her name left a weight on my heart. Hatred for Rose sizzled off my tongue like melted hot butter on popcorn. How could someone so cute, sweet and brilliant be an object of my hurt and hate? Whenever I said Rose's name all I felt was anger and I cursed her name. In my eyes she was a lazy poet full of talent but refusing to work a regular nine to five to support her poetry the way she should to become a success. Rose, the apple of my eye became the enemy from the black pits of hell and I wanted to destroy her for the sake of good and the sake of all mankind. I am not sure exactly when or why this happened but one day I snapped. I had become nameless, friendless and just in a terrible state of depression and mentally abused by Rose and her personal do me girl and mental slave. "Not me! Humph! Not Safari Ann Jones!" No matter how much I tried to fool myself I knew I was at the bottom of the bare, and at wits end. It was not a good thing to feel this way about Rose. I hated Rose Sutra so much that I began to retaliate. I began to mentally abuse her and my anger became rage and the rage became my fury. I was angry for all the times that I showed love and concern for Rose and she showed me her three quarter hind parts to kiss. I was angry for all the times I stretched my neck out to save her soul and she betrayed me and spoke to me like a dog. Rose lost my respect and I began to physically abuse her. I slapped rose and I punched, kicked and shoved her. My sweet nature had turned into an animalistic form of my former self as I metamorphosis from a sacrificial lamb to a full-fledged demon. I didn't know who I was anymore. Was I Satan? I started to feel that in the few months we had been together that my anger and resentment had been blending and brewing and churning through my veins like bad blood. Somehow dealing with Rose made me loose Safari in the jungle, who was I? Safari Ann Jones no longer existed and inside I was fighting with all my might to rip down those walls of hurt and pain that the devilish souls from my past has seared into my heart and mind forever. I felt like a vampire had sucked out my sweet and godlike soul and was trying to capture and destroy my body. My annihilation was inevitable and Rose was part of my demise. One night after a night of drinking and fun Rose's accusations caused me to just SNAP! Liquor in my system along with anger is like throwing a match in a tank full of gasoline and then putting your face in it as it blows up. I was enraged and at this point, I turned into the devils spawn full of anger and fury. I was ready to annihilate Rose as I began to have flashbacks of the abuse and torture that I endured at the hands of lesbian women who claim to love but have done nothing but hurt me. I could smell the evil in the air and Rose's accusations were me with countless blows to her face and blood splattering everywhere. My fists swung like the pickaxe of a serial killer and I felt no pain with each blow. I released ten years of pain and heartache that these women bestowed upon me. Rose screamed and cried for me to stop hitting her and I just couldn't. It was like I was possessed by a vile demon that enjoyed to see Rose in pain and the battering continued. Finally, I had my chance at revenge and I was having flashbacks of every ex girlfriend who betrayed me. With every blow to Rose's face I felt relief and it felt damn good! I laughed at Roses pain. I swear Satan had taken over my body and the whole experience felt like an out of body experience. Where was Safari Ann Jones? Where was the meek, sweet girl that knew nothing beyond church and the taunts of school children sent her home in tears everyday of her life? Safari was nowhere to be found. All of a sudden it was like, I had been battling an evil spirit for the possession of my body, and while fighting this demon, I finally managed to jump back into my body. It felt like a horrible experience with astral projection and suddenly, I was standing there watching Rose bleed at the responsibility of my slender brown hands. I was in shock when I saw her Carmel face bleeding. I offered her a towel. I felt shame and disgust for what I had done. I wanted to cry and tell her I was sorry, but my hardened outside wouldn't allow me to. Rose cleaned herself up and decided she wanted to come out and fight me, but I was too quick for her. Rose cursed my name as I silently ducked and dodged her potentially deadly hits. Finally, Rose snatched one of my things and I took one of hers. Like children we haggled and taunted each other. Finally, Rose grew tired of the nonsense and She decided to call the police. We struggled for the phone, and then I slammed it down. As I tried to gather my things Rose began throwing my things outside and proceeded to kick and stomp my things. I scrambled around on the ground and finally, I got everything into my car and swore that the relationship was over. I called hysterical and just wanting a shoulder to cry on. Well this so called friend of Rose's was no friend at all, she told me Rose was crazy and a psycho, and I should leave her alone, then hung up on me. I felt so mixed up and shaken that I put my head down and began to cry. My phone rang and rang. Finally, I picked it up. It was a police officer looking for me. The officer threatened to throw me in jail if I didn't return to rose's house. I was so pissed and crying all in the same breathe. I spoke to a friend of mine

Jobeth and she convinced me to go back and speak to the cops. I was so scared. I partially grew up in the south and I knew that being black and dealing with cops could be deadly. One wrong move and you are dead and gone on to glory. I didn't want to be on the eleven O'clock news starring as the body between the chalk lines, so I sat on the back of my car with my hands visible and I removed my jacket so that all of my slender body parts cold be seen. I told the cops my side of the story and I walked away that night feeling so hurt. I had hurt the woman that I loved. But, now I was going to have a police record because of my anger and her spitefulness. I had just started a new job. I slept in my car that night until it was time to go to work. I swear that was the longest day of my life.

Rose claimed that she dropped the charges, but I found out the cops dropped the charges for insufficient evidence. I was relieved. I had a clean background and I wanted to keep it that way. From that day forward, I never raised my hands to her or anyone else. Prison is not a pretty place. I learned that I better focus my energy and anger somewhere else or the slammer may just is my future home. Rose's jealousy had been the beginning of many arguments. We even auditioned for this television show called Starting Over. We were trying to save the relationship, but we didn't get picked even though we truly needed the help. So we went to a local couples counselor hoping to save our relationship. The counseling worked for a short while, but Rose sprung back into action and began accusing me of cheating on her.

I planned a trip to South Beach, Miami. We were supposed to have a loving and healing weekend together. We had a beautiful condo and the bed was huge and the kitchen was so pretty and shiny. We made passionate love that night and our souls reconnected. We made love on the beach and we got caught at least five times on the beach, in the open air but we didn't care our souls were united as one and the passion exploded from our bodies like fourth of July fireworks. The entire weekend was magical. This is what I always have wanted with Rose, peace and love. We went from club to club to party later that evening and there was this very attractive young lady, whom I must say was not my type but nonetheless was very pretty. She smiled at me, and I smiled back. I commented to Rose that she looked like this girl from Orlando that I knew. Rose's jealous rage started up again and Rose stomped out of the club, hopped in a cab and left me alone at the club and penniless. I didn't realize Rose left me at the club until my cell phone rang. It was Rose. Rose was yelling, cursing, calling me a whore, a slut and any other horrible name she could think of. Each word stung like a million stinging African bees in my ears and then I SNAPPED! I cursed Rose. I could be heard screaming at her for miles around. I was pissed the hell off! I told Rose to get out of my hotel room and that I was going to call the police.

Rose was in tears. She was on her knees begging me not leave her penniless and two hundred miles from home. I was so angry that I decided to play at her emotions. How dare she take my kindness for stupidity and then treat me like dirt beneath her feet. The next day, I left rose standing on a corner of South Beach with her suite case in hand and the look of anger in her eyes. I had only driven two blocks away and sat there for a while to scare her. Rose had her own agenda in mind. She lied and told me she had no money and according to Rose, she sold her poetry cd's just to get a bus ticket back to Orlando. Meanwhile, I was walking all over South Beach for four hours searching for Rose. I was in tears. I called the police to report her missing, but they just laughed at me. I walked until I was emotionally and physically drained. I cried my eyes out and I was scared and worried about Rose. A friend of mine told me to check the local bus station to see is somehow Rose hopped a bus home. Do you know that Rose hopped on a bus to Orlando and never called or said anything after I called her over and over on her cell phone begging her to call me and tell me she was ok. That was dirty and rotten of rose, and it serves me right for being mean first, but in this case we were both wrong even though her jealousy started it again. I vowed that never again, I would be the evil or mean to Rose. We both vowed to go back to counseling and try to fix this mess. I love Rose, and she loves me. The saga with she and I continues. Rose says she wants to marry me one day, when it is legal for gays to marry. In my heart my love for Rose is true and loyal, but if her jealousy and my rage cant stop then our love might some day be gone forever. Only God knows the answer to our future, but hopefully somehow our love will bring us through the rainstorm together.

FLASHBACK TO THE TIMES WE HAD

By Rose

Now gazing back, I am tripping on the fact that my birth mother died at the age thirty-two. I was also named after her. A really good horror story this could be! Sometimes I'm still tripping, "Why"? Because, I witnessed her deaf! I can remember that summer's day. I ran into room and my mother said, "Can you and Byron, my cousin, go walk Pretty." I went back to in the other room and told Byron, we had to walk the dog. That was the strangest dog walk I ever experienced. We both had walked pretty to an unusually place in the park. We were way in the back of the park. As we were walking Pretty, Byron and I saw this strange animal that looked like a half human and half lion. We did not know what we were seeing, so Byron, Pretty and I hauled ass! In other words we jetted. We ran and ran, until we reached the front door of our apartment in Harlem New York. As we reached the fifth floor, there were ambulance drivers, and nurses kneeling over somebody, and that somebody was my mother. I did not know what to say or do. The ambulance driver held my hand to move me back while they tried to give her "mouth to mouth." But not one breath could bring her back to life. The nurse yelled out, "DOA." I did not know what was going on. The nurse said, dose this lady have any children? The next-door neighbor said, she's standing right here. The nurse said to me, "Your mother is dead." I said, dead? The next-door neighbor grabbed our hands and led us in the apartment, and called Byron's mother and father to fill them in. Doreen and Jason came to pick us up, and take us back to Brooklyn.

Brooklyn New York was my new home now. And, all the drama that life had to offer. Jason was constantly beating Doreen's ass. I really hated seeing my aunt, whom I now called my mother getting hit by my uncle Jason, who I called my father. I would constantly jump in. As for my big head brother, he would either sleep through it or sit in his room and act like he did not hear anything. He was a little sucker. Yes, to this day I would not live with a man if someone paid me. I feel I would have flash backs of my mother being beat by my father and eventually kill whatever man I lived with. So to save myself from a lifetime jail sentence, I am choosing to be with women for the rest of my life on this planet Earth. Yes, my childhood has molded and shaped my adult life. But, I am presently working on changing and improving my attitude everyday. So when I flash back, I look at the most vulnerable time in my life, was when I sat in the holding cell before they ship your ass off to Riker's Island. As I was reading the prison walls I saw my mother's name Doreen written across the wall. I tripped the hell out inside my body, as I looked around me. There was a filthy cell full of women, with mice and water bugs crawling on the floor, we all were pushing and yelling for the bench to stand on. What really grossed me out was when this drug attic female picked up a cheese sandwich off the floor that sat by a big ass water bug and ate it. I was about to throw up. That's when I said to myself "This has got to be the gateway to hell!" And, I was surely right. Because the next day, when your handcuffed to other women, the prison guards led you through a corridor and up three flights of stairs and at the very top of the steps on the wall, reads HELL in red and black letters. From that day forth I was shitting brinks. I was handcuffed to a rowdy girl from Brooklyn. I wanted to die! I would never ever wish this experience on anybody. I cursed Lynn in my mind for putting me here. I was praying like crazy to be released from this nightmare. Freddy did not have jack on me! This was the true nightmare on Riker's Island! This was my wakeup call to never raise your hands to hit someone no matter what they do to you. Your ass will end up behind prison bars. I have learnt to walk away and wish that person well. This has been my greatest lesson on this planet Earth, to respect those that do you wrong, and by using nonviolence you will save yourself in the long run. I now use my mind to get what I want done, not my anger. No child should be raised in an environment where there is constant battlefield.

My second lesson that Riker's Island taught me was, that if a woman wants a hard dyke female, let her go find what she wants. You will never grow or amount to be what another woman wants or desires, if she continuously tells you to change to please her. From experiencing the lesbian life style, I must say, "Women are very fickle, selfish, self centered, and very devious." Women are more fucked then men. At least a man will cheat on you in private. You may turn the key to your door and there is your lesbian lover is making love to some other women, right in front of your face. I have learned my lessons. If someone does not except you for who you are, you can either keep that person as a friend or walk away. Seeing what a hard female really looks like after visiting Riker's Island, no thank you. I would rather be me. I am not hard or soft. I like what I like. If I cannot satisfy her, then I will walk away in a heartbeat. I have learned my lessons. I would like to live life now to it's fullest.

In conclusion, as for Safari and Rose, we will work it out, and stay together through thick and thin. So I thought, but I had to let Safari go. Why? She hit me first. When Safari hit me, it felt like I went into a twilight zone. I felt the pain of my mother being hit. I was finally getting over that childhood trauma, only to return to it again. Safari had some serious mental issues, based on alcoholism. Safari would blame me for not finishing her education. Yeah, I may have acted a bit too jealous about anyone other woman being around my mate, but that's me. I probably won't ever change in this lifetime. I really hope Safari gets over herself? I really fell in love her. The last poetry piece in the book is titled, "4 HUR." I wrote this piece for Safari. I remember rehearsing the piece in the living room of my apartment. Safari ran into the living room and said, "You are making me hot." So I stopped rehearsing and we made love on the living room floor.

My third lesson learnt, was not to stay in unhealthy relationships. No matter how much you think you love that person. It took me years to learn these essential lessons and a bloody nose! If you really love somebody, you will never raise your hand to that person. Domestic violence kills all relationships. Walk away before you raise your hand to that special person. Life is too short to waste. You know when you feel love for that special woman. Don't let a day go by without telling her that you love her. Women are the backbone to society. Without women, where would this world be?

FOR HER

By, Rose Sutra

In her eyes you often fanaticize…

In her eyes you now realize, that she is that woman

The apple of your eye,

The queen of your dreams,

The peach that you feign,

The love Jones that you desire!

The spark to your fire!

For her you would cross a thousand seas.

For her you would sell your last dream.

For her it's all or nothing.

For her you would bleed,

Your last breathe, your last touch, your last feel!

Tell me why does it hurt so much?

To have embraced you, to let you go once again…

I watched you as you walked away in perfect step as fashion models always do.

I truly believed in you.

I truly fell in love with you.

That's when I knew that I had to live without you.

Letting go of what was and now embracing the new, without you.

I am once again learning something new, learning to live without you.

Cum back to me, now…

www.ingramcontent.com/pod-product-compliance
Lightning Source LLC
Chambersburg PA
CBHW020132180626
46810CB00004B/1517